SILVERHEELS

Tara Meixsell

First edition
Printed in the United States of America

ISBN 1-809437-58-1
Library of Congress Catalog Number 2002100710

Western Reflections Publishing Company
P.O. Box 1647
Montrose, Colorado 84402-1647
www.westernreflectionspub.com

On the front cover: Photograph of Alma, Colorado, courtesy of
South Park City Museum, Fairplay, Colorado. Photograph of a
Victorian woman, courtesy of Colorado Historical Society.

Cover and book design by Paulette Livers ⁊
Livers Lambert Design, Boulder, Co

Acknowledgments

I thank the many people who helped me with various aspects of this book. Rose Hively, Glenda Emmans, Michelle Kingsford, Pat Creed, Margaret Fanning, and Pat Cody for their hours of assistance and encouragement; Dr Hutchinson of Salida, Robert Porter of the Summit Historical Society, and Carol Davis of South Park City Museum in Fairplay for all their help providing me with historical information. I thank Anne and Mike Meixsell, Craig Wilcox and Al Laurette for the patience and support they gave me while I wrote this book.

Special thanks to my editors Ann-Marie Flemming and Debbie Brockett for all their help and excellent editing of this book; to Paulette Livers for her wonderful design of Silverheel's cover and interior pages; and to publisher David Smith and Western Reflections Publishing Company for choosing to publish my first book.

ONE

IT WAS 1862 and Josie Pye, the striking dark haired young woman was running away, getting as far as she could from St. Louis and the man who had deceived her. She was traveling high into the Colorado mountains to gold country where she could start her life anew. She traveled by train from Saint Louis and finally boarded a stagecoach in Denver for the last and most rugged leg of the journey. The trip west had been rough and tiring, and Josie's body ached from the cramped seating and the constant jolting of the small coach compartment.

The stage made its way slowly through the heavy spring snow, not making nearly the time it would have on a clear day from Como, Colorado, to Buckskin Joe. From inside the coach, all that could be seen from the small frosted windows was a swirling mass of white with no beginning or end. The snow did not appear to be falling on the wide South Park plains as much as it was whipping in all directions at once. The fierce wind howled deafeningly and with great force, tossing the stage about and causing great fear and discomfort to the passengers within. The noise of the wind was so great it was almost impossible to talk, even to a person sitting just inches away.

Josie sat hunched against the wall of the stage as it lurched its way across the wicked winter of South Park. Her pretty face was contorted with sadness and her eyes were dull and sunken from crying. Her thoughts were as bleak as the world that raged on the other side of the window. Her near sleepless mind wanted to be blank, as blank as the swirling white mass that she stared into. The strange intensity of the storm put some fear into her, yet she really didn't care. She turned the brim of her large, fashionable black hat down low so it concealed most of her face.

Two nights ago, after arriving in Denver, she immediately made a few inquiries before purchasing one-way passage to the gold mining camp. The friendly railway porter assured her that Buckskin Joe was the site of the largest gold strike in Colorado.

As he helped unload her two suitcases from the train, he gave her a knowing look and said, "A pretty girl like you won't have no trouble findin' work up in Buckskin Joe."

Josie was too tired to care about his coarse remark, as she climbed aboard the stagecoach. She only cared about getting as far away from Horace as her money would take her. Maybe then she could forget about her love for him and begin a new life for herself.

The other stagecoach passengers murmured together, their voices almost soundless against the roaring wind of the storm. Often the stage would stop as the driver struggled to make out a form, a shadow, or any indication of the roadside. To those inside, the stops were almost imperceptible, as the coach lurched and swayed in the gale force winds. Josie barely noticed.

Her mind was far away, too close to Horace Greenly, the man she had loved for more than five months. How intense her feelings had been those first weeks of their intimate relationship! She remembered her newly discovered happiness, drawn to him as if her body had a will of its own.

Horace was almost twice her age, and he was the most handsome gentleman she had ever met. He dressed impeccably in a finely cut dark suit, and his clean, crisp white shirt was fastened with a thin black ribbon tie. Thick, dark brown hair curled away from his wide forehead beneath the brim of his expensive hat. His eyes were gray with the slightest tint of green. Like everyone who met Horace, she'd been struck by his intelligence and integrity. The first time they met, his gaze was so personal it seemed to pierce her very soul. Then and there Josie lost her heart to him. She'd believed that they were fated to be together. He was the man who would lead her into the mysterious world of adulthood. How foolish she'd been!

As she sat in the stage heading higher and higher into the Colorado Rocky Mountains, Josie could still see him turning away from her. Her face became hot as she remembered her despair as he had averted his eyes from her beseeching ones. It had been two weeks since she had last seen him on market day in the streets of St. Louis, and her mind had replayed it a thousand times since.

Horace was with his family, apparently out for a Saturday stroll or perhaps a bit of shopping. They appeared well to do. His diminutive wife was fashionably dressed as were the two small boys. They wore matching knickers and caps. Horace, as usual, was quite handsome with a distinguished air of money about him from his shining leather boots to his clipped mustache and well-brushed hat. The two boys were happily stomping through the muddy puddles on the edge of the street by the produce wagons, and their mother scolded them.

"Didn't I already tell you two to stay out of the puddles? You'll ruin your shoes! I don't know why we even bring you to town!"

Their father merely had to say a few words and the two boys, with their eyes cast to the muddy ground, answered in whispers. "Yes Father. No, we won't, Father." Then the family proceeded down the crowded street, each boy grasped firmly by his father's hands.

At that moment Horace saw Josie who was just across the street. As she stared at him, shocked and horrified, he averted his gaze and turned abruptly away.

Josie stood there, unable to take her eyes from his receding figure. Tears were swimming in her eyes, making her vision blurry. They began to run down her pale cheeks and trickle underneath her chin. The high-buttoned collar of her white blouse became sodden, but she took no notice. As his tall figure faded, so did her hopes of great happiness in the future.

They first met five months earlier when Horace went into Josie's mother's seamstress shop to do some business. Immediately he noticed the young woman who sat quietly stitching in a chair behind the counter. She was of medium height and slight build, with a face of delicate beauty and fineness. Her skin was pale under dark, wavy hair arranged in a loose bun. Within minutes he'd created a reason to ask her assistance and began a conversation with her over the price of various bolts of woolen fabric. He said he would return later in the day to pick up his order. Before leaving, he asked what time the shop closed.

At exactly three minutes to closing time he returned, and Josie was alone in the shop by then. After she gave Horace his bolts of woolen cloth and took his payment, Josie waited for him to leave so she could lock up shop for the night. He paused at the door with his hand upon the knob and looked at her.

"Is there anything else, Mr. Greenly?" Josie asked, thinking that perhaps he wished to purchase more fabric.

He looked steadily at her without turning the doorknob and answered, "Yes, there is one more thing. I wonder if I might have the pleasure of your company for a cup of tea. You are closing up now aren't you?"

Josie felt the blood rush to her face and she was somewhat flustered, yet at the same time flattered by the attention of such a handsome, well-to-do man. "Yes, I am closing up now. But I have to deliver a package, I'm afraid I can't accept your offer for tea." She darted a quick glance at him and smiled. He was indeed an attractive sort, and he also looked well educated, unlike the regular sort of men whose advances Josie took care to put off.

"Perhaps I could walk with you? It's a beautiful evening and I enjoy walking. Where do you have to go?" asked Horace.

"The St. Louis Seminary for Females, it's not too far from here. She paused for a moment, then said, "Are you sure you don't mind?"

"Not in the least, it will be a pleasure to accompany such a lovely lady. Besides, I can help you with the package," he said.

Josie took the cash box to the small back office, pulled the shades down, and locked the door behind them as they left. Immediately Horace insisted upon carrying the large parcel that was wrapped in brown paper.

"This is heavy! What's in here?" he asked.

"Costumes for the dance recital," said Josie. "Our shop makes all the costumes and uniforms for the seminary. They have a wonderful dance program. I enjoyed it so much when I was there." Josie was proud to mention her attendance at the seminary. It was a well-known and respected institution in St. Louis.

Horace was curious about Josie and wanted to learn all that he could about her circumstances. "When did you attend the seminary?" he asked.

"I began there when I was twelve, and I graduated when I was seventeen," she said. She did not mention the fact that her ability to attend the seminary was due to the fact that her mother traded seamstress work for the tuition bill. Josie herself had sewn stacks and stacks of costumes, uniforms and linens to help.

"Did you live at the seminary?" asked Horace.

"No, I lived at home. Most of the girls from St. Louis did. Only the girls from further away were boarders. I felt sorry for them because they only went home at Christmas and summer holiday," said Josie.

"I'm not at home much myself," said Horace. "I travel a lot with my work, I purchase and distribute soft goods. I've been doing it for so long now I'm used to it. I enjoy seeing different cities and not being tied down in one place like so many people are."

Josie glanced at Horace. He was the kind of man she had always dreamed of meeting—breathtakingly handsome, courteous, and by all appearances rather well to do! What a wonderful change he was from the young men who whistled and called suggestively to her when she walked down the street alone.

When they grew close to the seminary, Josie stopped.

"Mr. Greenly, it might be best if I deliver the package myself and meet you back here." Josie did not want to risk arousing curiosity at the seminary by arriving in the company of a man. Although she no longer attended, one of the Sisters might mention such an event to her mother.

"I will wait for you here," said Horace easily, as though it were normal.

Just a few minutes later, Josie returned. Horace took her by the elbow and steered her along the crowded sidewalk. She felt light on her feet although she had worked over ten hours that day.

"I shall take you to my favorite tea room. It is in a wonderful spot to watch the sunset along the river," he said, as they strolled along on the pleasant spring evening.

Josie felt drawn to this man as metal is drawn to a magnet. He held her arm close to his own as they walked, and Josie felt a tingling sensation travel throughout her entire body. They stopped and sat on a wooden bench beneath a weeping willow tree whose branches almost touched the ground. It formed a green curtain around the bench and in its shelter he kissed her. Her heart beat as rapidly as a wild bird's. He moved his face back from hers and looked intently into her eyes. She felt as though he could see her entire being, her mind, her body, and her attraction toward him.

He brushed a dark strand of hair from her temple, touching her skin with the back of his large fingers. "You are the loveliest girl I have ever seen," he said. "I could not stop myself from kissing you. I knew as soon as I saw you in the shop today that I wanted you."

As he said this Josie felt a strange heat rising through her body. He held out his hand, and she took it in her own. Silently they stood together beneath the great willow tree while the strands of leaves swayed about them like thick, green hair in the evening breeze. They walked back along the path they had taken beside the river.

"Because I travel so often I have a room at the hotel here in St. Louis where I stay when I come into town." They walked silently along for a while, then he said, "It was my good fortune today that I came to buy bolts of wool in your shop, and I can see that I will need to come back to St. Louis more often. Now that I've met you."

She drew her breath in sharply, and wondered at his words. It was too much to think that such a gentleman would be seriously interested in her!

As the sun sank below the horizon, the river's rippled surface turned golden. The swallows swooped in arcs above the water, catching insects before darkness fell. She and Horace talked of vague generalities, subjects of interest but with no real substance. When they came to the entrance of the hotel, Horace looked at her. Without a moment's hesitation, she followed him through the door.

Silently Josie walked beside him through the richly appointed lobby and took note of the velvet-covered chairs and dark oil paintings on the walls. Together they went up the narrow staircase toward his room on the upper floor. It was dark in the room, but he did not light any of the lamps. Instead he led her to the small sofa by the window and they sat down together.

"You are not frightened of me, are you, Josie?" he asked her.

"No," she answered honestly, "but I have never done such a thing before, coming to a room with a man."

He leaned over and kissed her, this time longer and harder than before. She felt his arms reaching about her, and she knew that she was not going to stop him.

~&~

IT WAS THE FIRST TIME in her young life Josie became involved with a man. Horace devised a clever plan-each time he arrived in St. Louis he sent a note to the seamstress shop inquiring about fabric orders. This was the agreed upon signal for Josie to meet him that evening at his hotel. He gave her a key to the room so that she might enter discreetly. He usually came to town on Monday or Tuesday because of his business route. That's what he told Josie, anyhow.

It was not difficult for Josie to get away to meet him, for she soon created convenient alibis for these secret visits. She wrote several letters to an old classmate, Harriet Finch, who lived on a farm outside of town. After passing several letters back and forth an invitation to visit was soon extended.

Josie also developed a sudden interest in assisting with the dance classes at the seminary, and she actually did attend quite a few afternoon sessions. She enjoyed helping the girls perfect their plies and jetes for the upcoming recital.

Josie's mother was pleased that her quiet daughter was taking an interest in social activities and stepping out into the world more often. It did the girl good she thought, and she noticed the new spring in Josie's step and the bloom on her cheeks. She herself had lived a stressed and harried life since the death of her husband three years ago. Between managing the shop and helping her sister care for their ailing mother, no time was left for pleasure. Every evening after closing the shop, Mrs. Pye hurried to the house they shared with Josie's aunt, uncle and two children to attend to her mother. She had little time to waste questioning her daughter's whereabouts-the thought never even crossed her mind.

Early one Saturday afternoon a note was sent from Horace. Josie was overjoyed by this unexpected occurrence. Not long after reading the message she said, "Mother, Harriet has invited me over for a dinner party tonight; some of the girls from school are coming in from out of town."

"That's nice dear," said her mother absently. Mrs. Pye was hurrying to reconcile the books so that she could leave.

"Josie, would you be a dear and close up for me tonight? I want to get home with the new medicine for mother; she's been so poorly this week."

"Certainly mother, I'll lock up carefully—you know I always do." Josie answered calmly, concealing the great excitement that she was feeling. Horace was here and she would stay the night with him!

Before sunset Josie arrived at the door of Horace's hotel room. It was not locked, so she knocked softly and went in. There he was, just rising to meet her.

"Horace!" she cried as she met his embrace. They hugged tightly, and Horace began kissing her on her forehead, cheeks and neck.

"Josie, you are so beautiful!" he said. He stopped kissing her and reached into his pocket—pulling out a small box.

"This is for you," he said, an expectant smile curving on his lips.

She opened the box and lifted out an ornate silver brooch, it was a rosebud on a stem.

"Horace, it's beautiful!" she said, feeling her love for him swelling within. Never had anyone given her such a fine gift! Impulsively Josie flung her arms around him and kissed him on the mouth. Horace lifted her and swung her through the air, laughing with delight as he deposited her gently on the bed.

And so began their first whole night together. It was a night that Josie would never forget.

This new life showed Josie pleasures that she had never dreamed existed, and she began to build her world around these wonderful nights with Horace. Although he was away more often than not, this did not bother Josie terribly because she was so in love with him. Whenever he was away she fed her happiness with memories of his handsome face and his touch. Alone in her small room she counted the days until they would be together again. And behind the fire of her love burned one small flame of hope—that he would soon ask her to marry him.

That hope was dashed in one fleeting instant when she saw him with his family. She was stunned to discover that he had intentionally deceived her, leading her to believe that he was a bachelor! All the stories of his business travels, his odd comings and goings—they were all lies! Most awful was the realization that the love between them was now changed; perhaps it had never truly existed. If Horace had really loved her, how could he have lied to her? Josie felt a stab of pain, as deep, as if a knife were being twisted in her heart.

After they had gone she stood in the crowded marketplace knowing she would not be with him again—even if he wanted her to. She had seen his children and his wife, and his evasive eyes. A numbing of all feeling came over her, yet she was able to lift her skirt hem from out of the mud and slowly make her way to the side of the street.

Turning her tear-stained face toward the building walls, she slowly walked back to her room as if in a trance. She slipped through the back door and hid her face with her hat. Fortunately no one saw her come in, and she went up the dark hallway to her room. Once inside, she sat on her bed and removed the pins from her hat. With the mud-encrusted boots still on her feet, she collapsed on the bedcovers and began to cry into her pillow, which she clutched tightly in her fingers. Although it was mid-afternoon, she did not exit the room until the next morning at 5:30 a.m.

Before the sun had risen enough to cast light through the windows, Josie made her way out of the darkened, silent house carrying two large traveling bags. She left a letter on her pillow, with a story that would serve as an explanation for her sudden departure. It would suffice for now. On her way to the train station she had to set the bags down often to give her aching arms relief. The one smaller bag filled with her books was especially heavy, as heavy as her heart. Her arms ached when she finally reached the station.

Josie left the bags near the loading platform and stepped up to the ticket window. After purchasing her one-way ticket to Denver, she sat upon the wooden bench to wait for the early train. She clutched her ticket in her black-gloved hand, waiting for the train that would take her away from St. Louis forever. She couldn't believe this was happening. She pictured his face again and again in her mind. It seemed to be all that mattered and all that she could think about. For more than an hour she continued to torture herself with those treasured memories of him. It was a relief to submit to the power of those feelings that she had neither the will nor the desire to fight.

When the train finally steamed in with a crashing and grinding of gears it was three minutes to seven. Josie rose and gathered her bags with the help of a porter and stepped aboard the train. As she finally sank into the seat which would be hers for the long journey, her eyes turned toward the window. She looked out on the town where she had lived for nineteen years. As the train pulled away with whistles screaming, Josie felt panic seize her. She didn't want to leave him.

The train settled into a rhythmic motion and the trees and fields on the outskirts of town whizzed by, and then fell behind when the train headed into the tangle of untouched woodlands. Alone in her compartment on the train, Josie thought of Horace and cried. The train rolled and clattered along taking her farther and farther from him and she remembered their last afternoon together in the small hotel, and how the fresh warm spring air had stirred the lace curtains in the late afternoon sunlight.

TWO

JACK HERNDON, OWNER of the Buckskin Joe Hotel, rolled over at first light and peered out his window below the curtain and groaned. Lying there in bed he closed his eyes and attempted to return to the comfortable land of sleep beneath the mound of woolen blankets and worn cotton quilts. Last night's fire had long since died and the cold air bit his nose as he poked it out of the quilts. Several minutes later he again lifted the patchwork curtain and looked outside. The snowflakes were large—slowly but steadily falling past his cabin window. The fresh snowfall was at least a foot deep, and the gray skies showed no signs of quitting any time soon. He could not return to sleep even though he wished to, for he had seen the light of day behind the snow and thick gray sky. His chores were waiting for him.

Swinging his long-john-covered legs over the edge of the loft where he slept he dropped with a thud to the floor. His dogs engulfed him, licking him and leaping upon his body, as he lay sprawled on the dusty floor of the cabin. "Hey! Get off!" he yelled as he swatted uselessly against the onslaught of canine greetings of the morning.

The snowflakes continued to fall steadily accumulating quickly as happens in spring storms. With little ceremony, Jack dressed in the rumpled denim pants and brown woolen shirt he had worn the day before that lay slung over the back of his chair. Making the one effort toward his appearance, he washed his face over the large white enamel washbasin filled with a mixture of water and ice bits. Taking up a scooping handful, he doused his face and wet the bangs of his thick, uncombed hair. Rubbing at his eyes, trying to make them open with the shock of freezing water, he continued to scrub his face with repeated scoops of water.

Refreshed and a little less puffy-eyed, Jack hastily dried himself with a thin piece of gray cloth that served as his towel. The cloth was gray with the dust and stove soot that were ever-present in the cabin. Mountain life was not meant for the fastidious. One soon gave up and resigned himself to a state of living close to the dirt and dust, as Jack had.

It was a constant round of daily chores, endless chopping, splitting, stacking and hauling of splintered logs, breaking the frozen ice of Buckskin Creek to dip out buckets of water for the barn, saloon, hotel and cabin; pitching dusty forkfuls of seedy grass hay into the feed bins, mucking the straw and manure off the barn floor and hauling it to the steaming pile out back. One never stayed clean for very long.

Once sufficiently washed, Jack pulled on his heavy coat and a pair of leather boots that were high enough to fend off all but the deepest snow banks. He found his gloves and hat and headed for the barn.

In the corral the horses stood together at the place where the fence was nearest to the cabin. They stared intently and hungrily at Jack's window. They had heard the sounds of waking in the house, the scratching and whining of the dogs, and waited expectantly for Jack to emerge and provide their breakfast as usual. As Jack caught sight of them he thought guiltily of the small pile of hay he had left out the evening before. If he had known it might snow he would have left them a bit more in the warm cover of the barn.

It was Saturday and business would be brisk at the hotel and saloon in Buckskin Joe. The stage was coming in from Denver, and the passengers would stay the night before leaving early the next morning for Breckenridge. Everyone, that is, except the inevitable group of men headed to the mines, full of hopes and dreams of hitting the mother lode. They too would fill the saloon and hotel, recklessly spending their last dollars on whiskey, so certain they were of the instant wealth to come.

Jack had seen countless bright-eyed, eager men head up the mountain to the mines and gold country, only to return weeks later in defeat. These men would pass in and out of the mining towns of Colorado by the hundreds. Upon their return to Buckskin Joe, they headed to the saloon after finding no fortune beneath the rocky soil, seeking refuge from their dashed dreams.

The saloon offered a haven, and for a while they could avoid having to face the future and it's uncertainties. With each gulp of whiskey the warmth cast by the oil lamps grew, and the comforts of the crowded saloon with its grand mirrored bar pushed all worries aside. For at least one night a man could put aside the harsh realities that awaited him tomorrow, when the last pinches of gold dust would be spent, and the whiskey would be transformed into a vicious cloud of a headache. The sickening of the heart would be matched by a sickening of the stomach, while waiting for the next morning's stage to take them away from Buckskin Joe.

Jack had seen so many of these men that he recognized the look in their eyes when they arrived in town. He knew what trail they were headed down as they swung their packs on their shoulders, following the burros laden with supplies up the dirt road which wound out of town beneath the tall pine trees to the mines. The louder and more boisterous of the men, the braggart and opinionated, seemed to fall to the deepest depths, get into more trouble, drink the most whiskey and leave town the quickest. Despite the often-freezing temperatures, it was not unusual to see drunken miners lurching down the alleys in their shirtsleeves, or passed out dead drunk in the doorways of buildings. When the light of morning arrived not all of these men would wake, and periodically a frozen, stiff body would be hauled away and buried with little ceremony. Some of the men merely came, tried, and failed, then left again for the unknown. Perhaps they went back east, or died, or moved onto yet another unknown territory where fortunes or devastation lay.

These men who were far from home looked with yearning eyes toward the warm-lit windows of the houses in town, while snow whipped down their collars on winter nights as they traveled from the mines to the saloons. A handful of these men might stay the winter and quit mining for the Company to work their own small claims. A few would switch to ranching and marry girls from one of the houses in town. What often started as a merry marriage party turned sour in the months of harsh mountain existence. Many a happily married miner found himself alone again, his wife long gone on some stagecoach to another life in the city, as far as she could get from barely scratching a living from the frozen ground and snow.

As Jack tended to his morning chores and prepared for the arrival of hotel guests from the stage, the snow continued to fall steadily, blanketing the rough frontier buildings and muffling sounds. One could barely see across the yard in such a blizzard and the first inclination was to return to the protection of the cabin and settle in close to the warm stove.

The hungry horses nickered and tossed their heads, pawing the snow at the sight of Jack. At the front door of the barn he cleared at least a foot of snow before he was able to swing it open. He went into the darkened interior of the barn. The inside was cave-like and sealed off from the rest of the world.

Jack shook the snow from his hat and coat and proceeded to pitchfork-load after pitchfork-load of the dusty, black seeded grass hay into the rough log manger. The horses crowded against each other in their rush for those first mouthfuls of hay. With her ears flattened back against her head the old bay mare lunged at the sorrel colt, biting him harmlessly on the neck as she secured her spot of dominance at the hayrack. Jack laughed at the rejected colt, pitching him a forkful of hay a safe distance away from the mare's teeth. "Ah, that's the tough life, Bud. Letting the old girl push you around still?"

Each horse ate from their own pile of hay, then settled contentedly with lowered eyelids to chew, ignoring Jack. The two dogs feasted on frozen chunks of horse manure in the corners of the darkened log barn.

"Now that's just plain disgusting!" Jack said to the dogs, who looked up at him briefly. They watched to see that he was not leaving, and then fell back to their chewing as Jack continued with his barn chores.

Now that he was awake, with the blood moving in his warmed limbs, Jack took pleasure in the morning. He liked the smell of the hay and the horses, the rhythmic sounds of chewing jaws, and the pleasant, familiar company of the animals. He thought of the strong hot coffee steaming in the pot at the bakery and the morning news to be discussed with a warm, fresh sweet bun in hand. After forking the last load of mucky straw into the bucket and dumping the mess onto the snow-covered manure pile behind the barn, he and the three dogs headed down the snowy road to the bakery.

⚭

THE WINDOWS OF THE BAKERY dripped with streams of condensed moisture from the heat of the large brick ovens. Jack Herndon sat with Tim the baker at a long narrow table near the stove and steadily drank cup after cup of steaming coffee.

"That stage is more than two hours late already," said Jack, as he poured a long stream of thick cream into his cup. "I wonder if they turned back to Como."

Tim was leaning back in his chair with his boots propped on an empty bench. "Have some coffee with your cream there Jack!" He threw back his head and laughed heartily. His brown eyes crinkled and he continued to chuckle as he poured himself another full cup of black coffee. "Ahhh," he sighed, as he stretched his arms wide.

"The Stage may have got into a bit of trouble. You know how that wind can blow out on the South Park. There was a time during those spring storms last year when I barely made it back alive. Couldn't see a darn thing just a foot from my face, I tell you. It was in that valley between Como and the peak to the south. Did they ever decide what to name that mountain yet?" He shook his head and frowned a bit as he said, "Sure hope Samuel got his stage back safe today."

Jack mulled these thoughts over as he chewed on a smooth sliver of pinewood from the kindling pile near the wood stove. "Hmm. Well, if they don't come in soon we'll have to send someone over to check at the depot. Of course, if a man were to get himself lost in a white-out, that's a danger too."

The two men continued to discuss the nasty spring weather and the late stage as they drank their coffee for the day. Both men were the pictures of mountain health. Their bodies, from their sunburned faces down, were lean and hard as wood. Both men's hands were cracked deeply and had palms as stiff as leather from the never-ending cycle of chores. Thick fingers more accustomed to freezing in wet gloves, gratefully held the hot tin coffee mugs. Most likely more coffee was consumed than a man really needed, just for the chance to hold the wonderfully warm cups a few moments more.

Both Jack and Tim enjoyed their morning breaks in the warm, high-ceilinged bakery, surrounded by racks of cooling bread while discussing the events of the day. It was one of those small but significant rituals that added pleasure to a grueling day.

A good amount of snow had accumulated on the muddy sidewalks of Buckskin Joe, and yet the storm continued to rage, whipping the tree-tops in its blind fury. Finally the stagecoach rolled slowly into town, six hours late. Horses and coach were encrusted in layers of ice.

The driver almost fell off his seat as he stepped down to unhitch the exhausted animals. He fumbled with the harness buckles. His frozen gloves refused to bend and his fingers were as useless as blocks of wood. The small door of the stagecoach swung open and out spilled the relieved passengers. Clutching their wraps about their heads in the gale force wind, they struggled through the bitter night toward the glowing windows of the hotel.

Upon hearing the muffled thud of feet climbing the hotel steps, Jack rose from his seat by the snapping fire and hurried to the door, holding it open wide for the frozen travelers to enter. The last person to enter was the driver, barely recognizable under a coating of white.

"Stage is out front, Jack. Can you come help me get unloaded? I can't unhitch my team, my hands are so frozen." He held up his gloves that were beginning to steam in the warmth. "We barely made it." After gasping these last words he collapsed onto the pine bench beside the fire, where Jack guided his fall.

Jack answered him quickly, "I'll get right out there Samuel. You stay in here and warm up." He paused for a moment before hurrying out and looked down at his friend in concern. "You've got to get those frozen gloves off or you'll lose your hands!" Jack leaned through the doorway that led to the kitchen.

"Kate! Come in here and give me a hand! These folks need some help fast for frostbite! Get some hot water for the driver. See he soaks his hands a good while. He might be in some trouble."

A pretty brown-haired woman appeared in the kitchen doorway. Kate was the hotel cook and housekeeper. She started working for Jack Herndon two years ago when she was twenty-one. She wore a dark blue cotton dress with the sleeves rolled to her elbows and a large white kitchen apron was tied about her waist. Upon seeing the slumped form of the driver, in addition to at least four more weary travelers near the doorway, Kate snapped into action. "Tommy, quick go fetch some water and put it on to boil! Get some wood on the fire in here; we've got to get these folks warmed up right fast! Hurry now!" She did not pause for an instant as she went from one passenger to the next, unbuttoning coats and wrestling stiff gloves from lifeless hands.

Jack hurried into his coat and went out into the blizzard. Holding his hands in front of his face to shield his eyes, he trudged toward the road. In the faint light cast by the hotel window, he could barely see the stagecoach and team through the blowing snow. The last passengers were getting out of the stage, fighting to hold the door open against the wind. Upon reaching the coach, Jack flung his weight against the door to keep it from closing. He reached out to help the last person jump down and grasped the small hand which was all he could see from his position behind the door.

"Jump!" He shouted as loudly as he could, trying to hear himself above the shrieking wind. "I've got you!" It seemed the lady belonging to the slight hand must have heard him because she jumped immediately. Jack held tightly to her hand, steadying her landing on the snowy roadside. But the woman did not land on her feet. Instead, she fell and lay crumpled in the snow bank.

In the darkness, Jack carefully gathered up the woman's slight body and carried her to the hotel door. Raising one boot while balancing the limp woman in his arms, Jack kicked several times as hard as he could against the heavy wooden door. Moments later Kate unlatched the door and peered out. She exclaimed in alarm, "Bring her in here! Careful through the door!"

She stood by him as Jack carried the woman through the narrow doorway. "Bring her upstairs to my room, then fetch the doctor!"

Once they had made it up the steep stairway, they laid her carefully upon the quilt-covered bed in Kate's bedroom. Kate undid the netting from the woman's large hat and began to unwind the long scarf covering her face. "Thank God! She's breathing!" Kate said, as she continued to loosen the woman's clothing. She paused before loosening the corset strings and turned to Jack, who was still standing in the doorway. "You had best go and bring Dr. Matson. I'll come back and check on her after I help the people downstairs."

Jack did not answer Kate. He was staring at the woman who lay on the bed. He took in her dark, wavy hair that framed an alabaster face-surely glad to still be alive. She was more beautiful than any woman he had ever seen. With one last glance, Jack disappeared through the doorway.

Downstairs again, Kate tended to the passengers with the competence of a nurse, taking matters well in hand as she relieved the pains of frostbite and soothed the nerves of the exhausted people with a gentle touch and a soft word. Her hair, once pinned in a neat bun, now fell about her face in soft, straying curls as she checked the boiling pots of water on the great cook stove. She continued to rotate hot, steaming water into the tin buckets, thawing the hands and feet of the people who were slowly recovering.

When Dr. Matson arrived Kate accompanied him upstairs. "Is anyone traveling with her?" he asked. Kate shook her head, "It didn't seem so, and no one claims to know her. They say she came up on the stage from Denver to Como."

The doctor rolled his sleeves up and began examining his patient. "Kate, may I have some hot water and soap please?" he asked. After checking the woman's pulse he pulled a stethoscope from his bag and fitted the earpieces to his ears.

Kate soon returned with a basin of steaming water and a cake of soap. "How is she Dr. Matson?" she asked.

The doctor turned to Kate and said, "Not too well off, I'm afraid. I believe she's miscarried, I'll know after I examine her." He plunged his hands into the basin and scrubbed his arms with the soap. After raising a good lather he rinsed and dried off on the towel Kate handed him.

Kate stepped outside the door while he worked over the woman. Finally the doctor called for her to come back in.

A pile of bloodstained cloths lay on the floor beside the bed. The basin of soapy water was also bloodied, Kate noticed.

"She's not bleeding too badly, the baby wasn't very far along. It must have just happened," said Dr. Martin. "She just needs to sleep now, and we'll see how she is in the morning."

The doctor gathered his things together and put on his coat. "Let's keep this between you and myself, Kate. It's an unfortunate thing."

"That's a good idea, Dr. Matson," said Kate. "I'll check on her tonight."

For the better part of the week the woman remained upstairs in bed while Kate nursed her back to health. While Kate cared for the sick woman that one of the passengers said was named Josie Pye, the hotel kitchen basically fell to ruin in the hands of Tommy who was just fourteen and not an accomplished cook. Tommy, more used to hauling water up from the creek and chopping firewood for the stove than actually cooking, served burned meats and watery soups that kept the regulars away.

During Kate's absence they took their meals at Buckskin Joe Saloon, the only other place in town where one could get a hot meal. It was a noisier and smokier environment than the homey dining room in the hotel, where Kate usually served up excellent meals of venison stew, fried trout, elk steak or other wild game prepared with her own English twist. People traveled for miles to savor such delicacies as Yorkshire pudding, Boston baked beans, and Kate's own secret recipe for chutney sauce. It didn't take long for the regular patrons to discover the joys of elk steak smothered in the rich, spicy concoction that Kate canned in jars by the dozen every fall when apples were delivered by the stagecoach from the valley orchards.

Each evening Jack paced back and forth across the worn pine floorboards of the dining room. His curiosity about the beautiful Josie Pye drew him there, and his restlessness overflowed to the chores. The wood box was piled high with split logs, and there was enough kindling for several weeks. Jack took every meal in the hotel dining room as usual, but lingered much longer than was his custom. He even began to read the newspaper after his dinner, and drank coffee in the evening as he sat with the stagecoach passengers in the soft chairs by the woodstove in the parlor.

There was no bar in the hotel, and those in search of a wilder sort of life would venture on down the road after dinner to find whiskey and a game of poker in one of the many saloons. After dinner it was Kate's custom to offer hot-mulled wine to the evening guests. She set a large cast iron kettle of wine and spices on the stove in the parlor and the sweet smell of cloves and cinnamon soon filled the room. A tray of metal mugs and a plate of ginger cookies were left on the table for visitors to help themselves. It was this kind of tender care that brought the patrons back to the hotel.

One night when Kate came downstairs from Josie's room she found Jack brewing a fresh pot of coffee in the kitchen.

"How is she doing today Kate?" he asked.

"Quite a bit better, now that her fever has gone," said Kate, setting her tray down and taking a seat at the table.

"She's eating now, mostly soup and tea." Kate leaned back in her chair and yawned.

"I am tired! These nights of being up with her have worn me out. It's a good thing she's feeling better-I need a good nights sleep!" Kate looked over at the stove and at the dinner things that Tommy hadn't put away.

"I suppose I better have some supper. What did Tommy fix tonight?" Kate grinned at Jack as she went to lift the lids off the pots. Both of them were well aware of Tommy's culinary shortcomings.

"Buffalo stew and beans, but something went wrong with the beans. First they were undercooked, so he put them back in to boil but all the water boiled off. The dogs didn't even want them. They were like little burned rocks," said Jack.

Kate dipped out some stew and tasted it.

"This is alright, it just needs salt." She sat down at the table, sprinkled the stew liberally with salt and pepper and began eating.

"Has the lady, I mean Josie, been talking much? Did you find out where she's from?" asked Jack in a deliberately casual voice. Actually, he was extremely curious about this Josie Pye. He passed a plate of bread across the table.

"Bread?" he asked politely.

"Thank you," Kate said as she took two slices.

"She's talked a little but hasn't really told me much about where she's from. I think at first she didn't really know where she was, and she was quite ill." Kate chewed the bread and thought about the secret that she and Dr. Matson shared. The less said about Josie's illness the safer it would be for the unfortunate lady.

"I'm sure when she's all well we'll find out more, but right now she needs to be left alone to rest. It shouldn't be too long now before she's better—that's what Dr. Matson said today," said Kate.

After a week, Kate left her vigil of caring for the sick woman upstairs and returned to her usual station tending the steaming pots on the cook stove. The news that the hotel dining room was up and running again spread through town, and at dinnertime that night the benches were packed with regulars seated elbow to elbow. The town's collective digestive system heaved a great sigh of relief.

～

FOLLOWING HER RECOVERY, Josie worried that her reserve money would soon run out. Many thought that Josie did not want for money because she had fine city clothes and fashionable expensive shoes. Actually these items had been gifts from Horace, and she continued to pay her expenses using the last of the money he had given her. Without ever saying a word to her, he had always left money on the dresser beside her hairbrush. Instead of spending it Josie had saved it and it soon amounted to a fairly tidy sum. There had been enough for the train ticket to Denver and the stagecoach up into the gold country. When she told Kate that she would be interested in working for her keep, Kate was more than happy to have her help. Things frequently got very busy in the kitchen, and even with Tommy's help, Kate could barely keep up.

As owner of the hotel Jack readily agreed to this new arrangement. He could not believe his luck! What an opportunity had fallen in his lap, to have Josie working right there at the hotel! Jack, who was not known to be prompt for meals, was now seen twice a day seated in the dining room like clockwork for breakfast and dinner. He sat at the end of the table nearest to the kitchen to get a good view of Josie as she came through the door to serve. When she happened to turn his way, Jack quickly averted his eyes and pretended to be deeply absorbed in the columns of the Fairplay Flume. He held the paper in front of his face at such an angle as to hide the movement of his eyes, as he followed Josie's every move around the dining room. His body tensed when she approached him with the coffee pot. This was his chance!

"Coffee, Mr. Herndon?" Josie asked, holding the pot poised to pour into his cup.

"Yes, thank you," Jack said. "How are you liking it here Miss Pye?" he asked.

"Very well, I'm glad I could work here with Kate," she said.

"She's happy to have you helping. Things get pretty busy around here. I guess you were just meant to come here," he said. What a beautiful woman she was, he thought again. Now that he was face to face with her she was even more striking—he had never seen blue eyes like hers. "Let me know if there's anything you need. We sure want you to stay." If only she knew why!

"Thank you, Mr. Herndon. That's very kind of you." She gave him a friendly smile before continuing around the table serving coffee.

After the meal was over and the opportunity to speak with Josie was lost, Jack kicked himself for not saying more. He could never think of the right thing to say until it was too late. After he left the hotel he carried her image in his mind all day.

Usually a no-nonsense and methodical worker, Jack found it difficult to stay focused on his chores. Several times a day he caught himself staring vacantly off at the distant mountain peaks, doing absolutely nothing at all but letting his mind ramble freely over thoughts of Josie. It didn't occur to Jack that he might be in love.

Jack wasn't inexperienced with women, he had just never been in love. In fact, there had been several local ladies of the evening who at various times considered Jack their regular customer and wanted him for their own. Not interested, Jack would fade quietly from the scene to a different sporting house. In Buckskin Joe there was no shortage of such houses. The large population of lonely single men working the mines kept the demand for prostitutes high.

Kate and Josie became fast friends. In their spare time their laughter could be heard from the parlor windows which had been pushed up to air out the stuffiness of winter with the warm spring breeze. Aside from Kate, no one else knew Josie very well. She rarely stepped across the threshold of the hotel to go into town. When she did, it was in the early morning when the streets were quiet, and she walked several blocks down the road to the Stone Church where she would disappear for a while. An hour or so later she would emerge and retrace her steps back to the hotel.

Although the curious townspeople tried time and again to get more information about this mysterious young lady, neither Kate nor Dr. Matson breathed a word of Josie's miscarriage. Personal information about her past and why she had chosen to stay in Buckskin Joe remained a question to all. The smaller the town, the more its inhabitants felt the need to know everyone else's business. In a larger city one had the hustle and bustle of the crowds to preserve privacy.

Josie made friends with the town children, and when the parlor door was open they knew they could come see her. Josie kept a glass bowl full of multi-colored sourballs sent up on the stage from Denver. Even the most timid child ventured over the threshold to select a piece, then whispered, "Thank you ma'am!" before fleeing back through the alley with the candy clutched tightly in hand.

Josie loved to see the children and felt most comfortable with them. She smiled in delight every time a child came into the hotel and asked for her by name. In a short time she knew each one personally, and they would often bring her a gift in return. Her collection included many lovely specimens of quartz, some with streaks of a dark rose color running through their milky depths. These stones lay across the window ledge in the hotel kitchen where Josie could see them while she helped Kate with the cooking. On her bedroom dresser she displayed a small bottle that held the feathers she had received. There were large orange and brown speckled feathers from the tail of a hawk as well as small pure blue feathers from a blue bird.

Josie accepted these gifts from her young friends as if they were more precious than gold, examining the treasures closely, exclaiming in delight. If there was time enough, Josie would read them stories from her fat, worn green book. They gathered about her feet as she led them into a land of castles, dragons, and knights. The smallest children boldly climbed into her lap and nestled there as she read. The affection between them was mutual. Josie tousled their hair and dispensed hugs all around, receiving sweet, sticky kisses on the cheek in return.

The days rolled into weeks as Josie settled quietly into the routine of life in the boisterous mining town. As spring turned to summer, the townspeople of Buckskin Joe began to accept Josie as one of their own. Only Jack was unable to voice his true feelings. He was still too tongue-tied.

The last Saturday morning in June couldn't have been finer. The fresh aspen leaves glowed yellow green against the dark pines. The slightest breeze set the leaves to dancing, a trembling canopy as far as the eye could see.

On such a beautiful morning it was hard to recall the deep blanket of snow that had so recently covered the ground during the last snowfall. When warm weather arrived so late, it seemed winter turned to summer almost overnight. The townspeople embraced the sudden warm season with even greater joy than usual. Dogs lay about the yards in the warm dirt as though dead, happily passed out from the effects of the hot mountain sun. Horses, too, stretched out lazily in the greening pastures near town, soaking up the wonderful heat with their great bodies. The cats enjoyed the sunshine more discreetly, resting beneath the cover of garden plants, watching always for danger.

Precisely on time, the stage came up the hill, arriving from the last stop it made in Alma about two miles back. Kate heard the customers in the dining area announce its arrival, and she put her head out the kitchen window to see. There it was, clattering and crashing along as usual, in a cloud of dust. If the street wasn't snowy or muddy, it was sure to be dusty. The large stagecoach raised such a cloud, only the driver and the luggage rack piled high with trunks and boxes were seen clearly.

For Kate the arrival of the stage meant the arrival of business. She quickly wiped her hands on the clean white flour sack that hung above the sink and then hurried through the front door. She prepared to meet her customers as usual, with a warm and friendly greeting.

As the driver pulled the team to a stop at the hitching post, he gathered the thick reins in one hand and tipped his worn hat graciously toward Kate. "Good day, Ma'am," he said smiling widely.

Kate smiled and nodded her head in return. "Good day, it certainly is nice that summer has arrived, isn't it?"

Although he was a tall, broad-shouldered man, the driver jumped down from his high seat easily. He seemed to be very fit and agile for such a large man. After hitching the team to the post, he helped the passengers climb down from the coach. Kate held the door open and greeted the guests as they entered the hotel. Once the team was secured the driver walked quickly up the porch steps toward Kate with his large hand extended.

"I'm Samuel Grey, ma'am. I do believe it was you who saved my life the night of that blizzard last time I was up. I'm indebted to you for that ma'am and have been wanting to thank you."

As he said this, he gripped Kate's hand tightly in his own, and gazed intently into her eyes. Then he smiled his warm smile again and went down to the coach to unload the trunks. Kate looked back at him with interest.

"You must call me Kate, Samuel Grey. Everybody does!" she called to him.

He stopped lifting down trunks from the luggage rack for a moment and turned to her saying, "That will be my pleasure, Kate!"

Soon each one became absorbed in the familiar tasks of their respective jobs, but it was possible that their minds were somewhere else altogether.

Kate first came to America when she was seventeen. She grew up in the outskirts of London in a working-class family. Her uncle, who worked on a ship which transported cotton from South Carolina to England, was able to secure a job for her as a cook on a plantation in Charleston. Kate eagerly accepted the offer. Her passage to America would be paid for in exchange for a three-year commitment to work. Knowing that only long hours in miserable conditions at a factory job awaited her in England, Kate's parents signed the working papers for their eldest daughter. They could barely support a family of three as it was, and having one less mouth to feed would ease the burden greatly. More nights than not, the family went to bed hungry in their small, cold apartment.

Shortly before Kate's indentured service was up, fears of war between the North and South grew. Joining hundreds of others, the plantation owners fled Charleston, taking Kate and several other household servants with them to New Orleans. There Kate met her uncle Joseph, and the two decided to head west in search of a new life far from the impending threat of Civil War.

That is how Kate came to Buckskin Joe. It was the year when a rich vein of gold was discovered off a branch of the South Platte River. Jack Herndon had been one of the first to set up business in the new frontier town, opening both a hotel and a saloon. As word spread of the riches of this lode, hopeful men arrived in droves.

During her first meal at the hotel, Kate inquired about work. At that time the building was merely a rough shell, with a dirt floor, open holes for the windows, and mud chinked log walls. At night blankets were tacked up over the window openings to keep the snow and cold out. Jack hired her immediately to cook for the hotel. He had far more business than he could handle due to the influx of hopeful miners.

From the start the arrangement worked out well. Kate took over all kitchen duties, leaving Jack free to attend to the many chores. Improvements were made to the building, glass windows were installed, a wooden floor was laid, and the walls were chinked with plaster. The hotel and saloon stood next to each other, separated by a narrow alley. In addition to her pay, Kate was given her own quarters on the second floor of the hotel. Kate had purchased a floral patterned cream and light blue wallpaper for her three rooms. It had taken quite a few months of her first year in Buckskin Joe to save the money for such an extravagance, but the sacrifices she made by wearing her worn shoes an extra six months and forgoing the purchase of a new dress was well worth it. Once the precious paper had been purchased and delivered by mail, she'd hung it carefully using flour paste, and tried not to leave wrinkles.

Whereas reading had never held much of an attraction for her as a pastime, sewing did. Kate spent many an evening in the pleasant surroundings of her own chambers contentedly sewing aprons and small linens while enjoying a cup of hot tea and a purring cat on her lap. She enjoyed the solitude of her rooms, a welcome change from the constant clatter and bustle of the kitchen after a long day's work preparing and serving meals. Kate found it rejuvenating to sink down on the overstuffed sofa in her sitting room, prop her aching feet on a pillow, and bask in the comfort of the haven she had created in the middle of a rough and raw mining town.

She was overjoyed to finally be independent and free from any obligation to an employer. Although she had been treated decently enough, her time in Charleston had seemed an eternity.

From the beginning Kate was careful to avoid the advances of the women-hungry men who found the lively young English girl attractive. She was not about to become the property of any man, no matter how charming he might appear. For the first time in twenty-one years Kate had control of her life. She had food, lodging, the means to acquire some savings, and the freedom to come and go as she pleased. The caged bird had finally been released. Romance, she decided, and the potential traps that accompanied it—could wait. But that was before she met Samuel.

After the arrival of the stage, the flow of people increased steadily on Main Street, as miners, townspeople, and visitors went about their business. Kate barely had time to catch her breath in the next three hours. The rush to prepare for the mid-day meal immediately followed the clean up from breakfast. At five minutes before noon Kate unlatched the front door of the hotel and stepped onto the porch. She unwrapped the kitchen apron from her waist and tried in vain to secure a wayward strand of brown hair behind her right ear. The hair had been swinging before her eyes most of the morning, a common annoyance. With a tired sigh she rested her weight against the railing of the porch as she took in a moment of fresh air and sun before returning inside to serve lunch. Taking a long piece of iron from the nail hanging off the rafters, she gave the iron bell a few hard whacks, the clanging resounded loudly throughout the center of town.

Almost immediately people began to appear, emerging from various doorways or alleys, all heading to the hotel dining room for their meals. These were Kate's regulars. Almost all were single men employed in town together with a few miners down from the diggings for a day or two.

There would be no more rest breaks, she knew, until the meal had been eaten and cleared, the dishes and pots washed, and the tables wiped clean. She was almost through the door on her way back to the kitchen when she felt a hand on her arm. She turned in surprise and found herself face to face with Samuel Grey.

"Kate, I would like to ask you to come for a drive up to Kite Lake this afternoon. I've heard that the columbines are finally coming into bloom." Samuel's hazel eyes smiled down at her in hopeful expectation.

"Why, I would love to!" Kate exclaimed, but her excitement quickly turned to disappointment. "Oh no, I couldn't actually, much as I'd like," she said more slowly. "You see I have the kitchen to attend to." She met his gaze full on, not afraid to look meaningfully into his eyes. With regret in her voice she continued. "But I certainly do thank you for the invitation."

She felt her cheeks get warm, and looked away from him. Thoughts of her one serious suitor, who had left town over a year ago, had suddenly come to mind. She'd believed his intentions had been serious toward her. They had talked of acquiring some land for a ranch far out on the South Park where the grass hay grew deep.

The memories always made her sad because she had lost something without ever knowing why. Kate looked brightly up at Samuel and said in a more hopeful tone, "Perhaps if you were able to come about three o'clock, I could get away for a bit before dinner."

Samuel carefully placed his brown, weather-beaten hat upon his head and bowed slightly. Touching the brim of his hat, he said, "At three then!"

With that, he strode off the porch and headed up the hill toward Jack Herndon's barn under the tall pines. Kate stood at the door of the hotel as the lunch guests began to file inside past her and watched his receding figure. The excitement of this impromptu adventure took hold of her mind. She breathed in deeply. There was no denying it. Samuel Grey was truly a handsome man. And a gentleman too, it seemed.

After a short search, Kate found Tommy asleep in the pantry on a pile of empty flour sacks. The boy loved to nap. He had acquired the habit when living with his father who dragged him along while he drank and gambled the nights away in saloons. As a result, Tommy was able to fall asleep almost anywhere when an opportunity arose. Kate shook Tommy by his shoulders to wake him. "Tommy, Tommy, wake up!"

In a moment Tommy looked up at her, bleary-eyed and confused. After sitting up and yawning widely with a great stretch of his arms, he slowly came to his senses. "What is it Kate, am I late for dinner?" He peered at her through sleep-messy hair that hung over his eyes.

Kate laughed and said, "No, no, Tommy. You're not late, I've just a favor to ask of you."

Fully awake, now, Tommy waited expectantly.

Kate spoke again. "I've been invited on an outing, and if you would be willing to help with the lunch clean-up I can leave for a few hours before dinner."

Tommy answered without a second's hesitation. "No trouble at all. You can count on me, Kate." Then he gave her a shy smile that Kate knew would someday melt a young girl's heart, for underneath his rumpled hair, Tommy was a very pleasant-looking boy.

Kate had taken Tommy under her wing three years ago when he first came through the hotel door with his drunken father. He was nearly starved, and the clothes he wore were filthy and ragged. When his father left town several days later he was so drunk he didn't even remember he had a son. Tommy was happy to have been left behind, and he hoped his father would not come back for him. Once she became aware of his situation, Kate provided the boy with a bunk behind the kitchen pantry and all the food he could eat. In return Tommy thankfully performed kitchen chores from dawn till dusk for Kate, such as chopping and stacking wood for the stove and hauling endless buckets of water up from Buckskin Creek.

Even at the young age of ten, Tommy had proven to be an enormous help to Kate in the hotel kitchen. Previously Jack, who owned the hotel, had seen to it that Kate always had a ready supply of dry, split wood stacked high in the wood box beside the stove. Tommy took that a step further. Every morning, somewhere near the hour of five, Tommy carefully placed small pieces of kindling wood in the large wood stove and coaxed the sleeping embers back to life, blowing on them gently. Every night before going to bed Tommy repeated this process to keep the fire burning until dawn.

In such ways Tommy demonstrated his devotion to Kate, and sometimes he ventured a small smile when she praised him for his work. Kate always returned his smile warmly and felt maternal stirrings within her for this young, abandoned boy. As time passed, Tommy became extremely comfortable with his new life in Buckskin Joe, enjoying the stability of a permanent home and the company of such kind people as Kate and Jack. The three of them were something of a family there at the hotel and kept things running smoothly and happily enough.

As she flew threw her chores at twice the usual speed, Kate's mind raced. To be asked out for a drive so suddenly by a gentleman! Samuel Grey spoke to her as if she were the finest lady in town, even though she was just a hotel cook. Kate pinched herself to see if she really was awake. She was so excited she barely noticed the food she was preparing for the evening meal. As she peeled potatoes she was thinking how handsome a man he was with his broad shoulders, dark thick hair and friendly sparkling hazel eyes.

Whereas some of the rough men Kate ran into in Buckskin Joe frightened her, Kate felt not a speck of fear toward this man she had so recently met. Never did it cross her mind to be cautious about going alone with him for a ride up into the mountains.

At precisely three o'clock Samuel pulled his groomed team to a halt at the hitching post of the Buckskin Joe Hotel. Graceful as a buck, he jumped from the high driving seat of the coach to the ground. Kate was ready when she heard his footsteps on the porch. As she went out the front door, her eyes met his. Samuel reached out his large, strong hand and grasped hers firmly, never taking his eyes from hers.

"Are you ready, Kate? I'm so glad that you could come with me today!" He released her hand slowly and then nodded toward the steps. "After you, ma'am."

They proceeded toward the coach and team of handsome bays whose well-brushed coats shone like gold in the sunlight. For this outing, even the harness buckles and bit rings had been polished to a sparkling silver. Kate felt very special.

Kate accepted Samuel's hand to climb up into the driver's seat, and he hopped up after her. He gave a shake of the reins and they set off at a brisk trot into the tall pine forest above Buckskin Joe. It was three miles up to Kite Lake. Kate moved a bit closer to Samuel as they bounced up the rutted road and leaned slightly against his arm. A few high clouds floated above the mountain peaks, framing the sun that still stood high in the bright, blue sky. It was a perfect afternoon for a drive.

Just a few pleasant and winding miles up Buckskin Road which followed along the wide rushing creek, the forest ended and one entered the high meadows of the mountains where the wildflowers grew thick in brilliant displays of color. High rocky peaks rose above the valley, where the glaciers were melting. Even in the summer the snowfields, patches of dwindling white upon the gray and yellow rock, still blanketed the high country. The streams gushed noisily due to the heavy snowfall from the winter. The stream bank could not keep up with the surplus, allowing stray water to form small lakes and ponds in the meadows.

Kate held onto her straw hat as Samuel drove his team of bays through these summer fields and up past the busy mines with their stained piles of slag where the orange streams ran from the mining waste. Just beyond the London Mine lay a beautiful narrow mountain valley where the abundant wildflowers were coming into their peak in all shades of the rainbow.

Here Samuel pulled the team to a halt. He came around to help Kate off the high seat and offered her both his hands. "Jump!" he said merrily. "I won't let you go!" He took her hands in his and swung her down to the ground beside him. Kate stumbled a bit as her feet hit the uneven tufts of meadow grass. She fell against Samuel's arm, but he still held her two hands firmly in his.

Her hat was knocked off her head down her back and dangled by its strings. Kate felt warm as he whispered her name in her ear. She leaned her head against his broad chest while he wrapped his strong arms about her. She breathed in his smell, a mixture of wool, horses and sweat. It was a most wonderful smell to her.

The close mountain peaks of the Continental Divide towered above them, and the sun sparkled off the rippling waters of Kite Lake at the narrow end of the valley. At that moment Kate felt a surge of happiness, and they remained still for some minutes, taking in the beauty of the place. Kate felt the unfamiliar yet welcome closeness of Samuel's body against hers. She closed her eyes for a moment. She did not want to let go just yet.

After a while the two walked through the meadow of brilliant flowers, stopping occasionally to discuss the names of the various plants and inspect their beautiful blooms more closely. There were white, orange and maroon Indian paintbrush, exotic columbine of white, blue, red, and purple, mountain bluebells perching on long graceful stems, and daisies of several colors.

Down at the lake at the point where the stream came in, there was a large marshy area carpeted with tall, midnight blue larkspur. Each flower had a tiny white star in its center. All along the stream grew bunches of the delicate white columbine-all the way up to the place where the spring bubbled up from beneath the rocky slope. Kate and Samuel walked completely around the lake, getting their feet wet as they crossed the stream. Eventually they rested on a dry stretch of meadow grass, and talked as the sun continued its journey across the western sky. They held hands and leaned on their elbows, talking easily as if they had been friends for years.

Down in Buckskin Joe the heat of the summer had reached its peak, and the sun bleached the rough-hewn boards of the town buildings to gold. Josie walked back to the hotel after her daily visit to the church. Even with the shade from her large brimmed hat, the sweat glistened on her face. She was overheated beneath the cotton summer dress, which covered her from chin to toe. The privacy of her room at the hotel beckoned to her. There she could unbutton the stifling hot collar and feel the breeze from the window against her hot skin.

It was days like this when she envied the men who could roll up their sleeves and enjoy a more relaxed attitude regarding attire. This evening, when Kate returned from her drive, Josie would ask to borrow her sewing pattern for an open-neck blouse so she would have something more comfortable to wear while cooking.

Sleeping dogs lay in shady corners along the roadside with their bellies pressed against the cool ground to help relieve the worst heat of the day. In spite of being frigid in the winter, the Colorado mountains could be hard to endure in the summer heat. A woman had a difficult time keeping the summer sun from burning her face and turning her skin dark like an Indian's, no matter how hard she tried to avoid the sun by hiding beneath hats and parasols.

Josie did not carry a parasol; she had left hers back East with many of her delicate belongings. Such things were easily broken along the long and rugged trip west. Besides, what used to be so special to her, such as her treasured teacup collection, had become faded memories of another time and place.

Josie stopped near the outskirts of town and stood on the side of the road for a moment, looking out into the forest up toward the mountains. The beauty of the mountain summer had struck her. She noticed the brilliant array of wildflowers and the soft grass with long purple seed heads like hair that grew out of the muddy roadside ditches. A pair of ruby throated hummingbirds with backs of shimmering emerald green buzzed by her then looped high up into the sky before diving down again.

She could hear the noisy gush of water from Buckskin Creek where it ran under the pine trees behind the hotel, and she smelled the wetness in the air. High above everything, the black rocks and white snow of the mountains accented the deep blue sky. It had happened, just as it did to most people who stayed a summer in the high country. Josie had fallen in love with the mountains.

Down the road the doors of the bakery were flung open to the breezes. Despite the heat of the day Tim sat resting against the front wall of the building on the small covered porch with a steaming cup of coffee in his hand. This was his regular break time after he mixed the dough for the night's baking. The town was unusually quiet at this hour; the miners were not yet down from their diggings for the evening.

Tim's all too short moment of rest was interrupted suddenly by the noisy clatter of footsteps upon the porch.

Tommy cried, "Tim, Tim! Come quick! Jack's horse, Buddy, is dying! He got into the grain bin!" Tommy barely stopped to relay this frantic message, and then he was off again running up through the trees toward Jack Herndon's barn.

Tim leaped to his feet and ran after Tommy. It was a short run of no more than a minute or two through the scrubby pines and thin aspens on the twisting, dusty path. The loud sound of a shot resounded through the woods. When he came close enough to see the corral he noticed Jack Herndon kneeling beside the body of his red colt. Tim stopped. The rifle that had just been discharged now lay in the dust beside the horse.

Tommy hovered anxiously behind Jack, his young face contorted in agony. Jack's eyes were fastened upon the young horse, whom he petted gently and slowly as he whispered softly, "Buddy, Buddy, my boy, Buddy."

Jack knelt in the dirt beside the large dying colt who lay sprawled on his side. The horse breathed a terrible gasping breath and then slowly another as his eyes rolled back and his stiffened legs shuddered. Then he was quiet. "Buddy, oh Buddy," Jack whispered to his horse as he petted his still cheek gently, not ready to accept his death.

He bent his head in sorrow as he sat beside his dead colt outstretched upon the ground in the corral under the tall pines. He did not notice the people clustered about, and their words went by him. He gave no answer to their questions but stared briefly and blankly at them as they spoke. He stroked his horse's beautiful young, strong neck as he sat beside the body in the growing dusk.

Slowly the group dispersed after awkwardly conveying their condolences, leaving Jack alone with his grief and with Tommy. Eventually Jack lifted his head and said, "There was no saving him, Tommy. He was dying of a twisted stomach, it was better to stop his pain. When they're down and rolling that bad you can never get them up again."

The two sat together beside Buddy's warm body, too overcome by grief to even cry, until the sky had darkened into almost total blackness except for a few stars that shone between the clouds.

THREE

FOR THE NEXT WEEK Jack did not even take one meal at the hotel where he had been a regular three meal a day diner since the arrival of Josie Pye. The faded patchwork curtains of his small cabin remained closed, but in the darkness of the night one could see the weak wavering light of an oil lamp burning inside, often far past midnight.

Although Jack had never been an outgoing man, his friends and neighbors were shocked and worried by the sudden change that had come over him since the colt had died so tragically. Each day as he went slowly from his cabin to the barn he walked with the gait of an elderly person—the soles of his boots barely clearing the ground. When he was spoken to, his eyes remained remote and his answers to questions were mumbled. Jack seemed uncomfortable around anyone except Tommy, who spoke very seldom himself.

The night that Buddy died, Tommy crawled into the hayloft and rolled tightly into a ball, crying into his woolen scarf to muffle the sound of his grief. The next day he went out into the corral but only after the stiffened body had been hauled off by two cart horses far out into the woods. The carcass would be left for the wolves. Tommy couldn't bear to watch. He stayed with the old bay mare, Ty. His tears leaked into her black mane as he hugged her neck and wept.

Ty seemed remorseful, too, looking over the fence into the woods where they had taken Buddy's body. She stayed near the place where he had died, sniffing at the ground. It seemed that she was looking for the young horse as though he might come trotting back at any moment. Horses are herd animals by nature and do not like to be alone. Every day Tommy spent extra time with the old mare, just standing near her and leaning against her, running his hands over her sleek hide. It made them both feel a bit less lonely to be together in their sorrow.

Just after breakfast in the hotel kitchen, Kate sighed as she brushed a strand of wavy brown hair out of her eyes. Josie had helped her clear away the dishes, and now they were having tea. "I'm getting worried about Jack. It's been over a week since Buddy died, and he looks no better. I wonder how we can help the poor man. That colt meant the world to him. He's been working with him for two years to replace his old horse. It's such a shame." She glanced out the window toward Jack's cabin under the tall pines. His door was shut.

Josie looked at Kate as she stirred her tea. After a moment's thought she said, "Perhaps we could bring him some dinner, maybe some stew?"

At this suggestion Kate's eyes brightened. "Oh Josie, that's a wonderful idea! Jack does love our stew; he always eats several helpings when we serve it for dinner. Why, that should certainly help to cheer him up!"

Kate began to move about the room, getting ready to go back to work after the tea break. "Let's start now, shall we? There's still enough time if we hurry..." She paused before heading into the narrow pantry for potatoes and said, "Josie, would you please come by the kitchen just before the rush starts and take the food to Jack? She looked at Josie for a moment then continued, "I think Jack has taken a fancy to you. Have you noticed the way he pretends not to look at you?" She grinned as she teased, "Perhaps you're just what the doctor ordered!" Then Kate disappeared into the pantry, leaving a flustered Josie sitting alone at the kitchen table with her cheeks burning.

As evening set in, Josie tapped lightly on Jack Herndon's door. She put the steaming covered pot of stew on the ground and knocked again, this time a bit harder. She could hear a rustling noise inside and then the door opened, showing a darkened and somewhat disheveled room behind.

"Yes ma'am?" Jack said, as he looked out at her standing there in the fading daylight. "May I help you in some way?"

Although he was polite, he stood a bit behind the door and looked at Josie dully. She was shocked by the dramatic physical change in the man, the dark, puffy circles under his eyes and the hunch in his posture. Jack Herndon was certainly not anywhere near as old as he looked at this moment. Yet, old he looked.

For a moment Josie stood and just stared. She held up the stew pot. "Why, Kate has made you some stew, the stew you like so well!" Seeing that he wasn't going to shut the door in her face, she became bolder. "It's nice and hot still. Shall I set it on the stove so it stays hot for your dinner?" She bent over and began to lift the pot of stew, but Jack stepped out the door.

"Let me help you, ma'am. You'll have to tell Kate thank you." Then he took the pot and set it on top of the small black iron stove with the fire showing orange red between the thin cracks around the door.

She stood in the doorway taking in the details of Jack's cabin. The small kitchen was comprised of a shelf of tin dishes, and several iron skillets and pots hanging from nails above a narrow wooden counter. The wash bucket was tucked beneath. A few supplies were stored on a second shelf—several cans of fruit, a tin of biscuits, and a jar of molasses.

On the opposite side of the room there was a crude bookshelf nailed into the wall that held a number of worn volumes. An assortment of tools, traps, and lanterns hung from nails driven into the mud-chinked cabin walls. A large piece of oiled canvas had been nailed down into the dirt to create a floor. The sleeping bunk in the corner was unmade, with wool blankets and quilts heaped in disarray. The cabin was distinctly masculine, but aside from the unmade bed it was neat and efficient. Josie liked it.

Jack turned toward her and pulled one of the chairs out from the small wooden table, "Would you like a seat ma'am, and take a minute with me?"

As he spoke, Josie noticed a steady thumping from beneath the table. Seconds later a white and black speckled nose poked out from beneath the faded cloth which covered the table.

Jack took a seat opposite Josie and said, "That's my dog Nipper under there. Suzy is hiding under the bed, she's a bit shy of strangers." Nipper seemed happy to see Josie and nuzzled her hand. Josie caressed the soft furry head.

When Jack found himself looking into Josie's blue eyes, some vague feelings stirred within him as he recalled that this was the woman he had so desired to meet just a few short weeks ago. And now, through no effort of his own, here she sat an arm's length away in his own cabin! Maybe some good would come from Buddy's death after all.

Jack lowered his gaze to the tabletop, and picked up a burned matchstick from the tin in which it lay. He snapped off the cleaner half, and used it as a toothpick. Jack's mind was racing in a direction that he felt compelled to follow; yet he remained paralyzed. He breathed deeply several times and attempted to calm his nerves.

When he looked at her again he noticed that Josie seemed to be equally flustered. Her high cheekbones were flushed red against her otherwise pale skin, and she clutched her hands on the table. Josie met Jack's eyes, with caution but also with interest. Her mind remained blank and she could not think of one word to say until the gentle thump, thump, thump of Nipper's tail brought her out of her silence.

With relief Josie turned her attention to the animal. She hesitantly extended her hand to the dog, and then asked "Is he friendly? May I pet him?"

Sensing the sudden interest being focused on him, the spotted hound poked his head out from under the tablecloth and looked as if he smiled at Josie, eager to make a new friend.

Jack laughed and said "Why, old Nipper there would more likely lick you to death as ever bite you, ma'am. He's as gentle as they come." He looked at her again, and this time noticed that the irises of her blue eyes were ringed with black, which made them look unusual. He couldn't remember ever having seen anyone with eyes like that.

Josie stroked the dog while he sat blissfully soaking up the attention with closed eyes. "What a sweet little dog!" she exclaimed. The dog thumped his tail wildly and nudged at Josie's hand, wanting to be petted again. Josie threw back her head and laughed, "I believe you would have me pet you all day, you silly dog!" Then she took the furry face between her hands and scratched behind the dog's ears.

"How old is Nipper?" she asked, all her self-consciousness forgotten after playing with the dog.

Jack chuckled, "That old boy is at least ten years old, I figure. He found his way to my door one summer day years ago and stayed. He thinks he owns the place now." Under the table, Nipper thumped the floor with his tail, seeming to know he was being talked about.

Jack rose to his feet and went to the wood stove to get the cast iron teapot. He wrapped a scrap of burlap sacking around the hot handle and carried the steaming pot to the table. Next he set two well-worn tin cups on the table. "I've some tea ready here ma'am. It came from Denver. Would you join me for a cup?"

Without waiting for a reply, he took the tea tin from the narrow shelf that constituted his pantry and measured a few spoonfuls into the pot. "It's real English black tea. That's the kind I like best. I'd just as soon go without than have the stuff they sell at the mercantile. I don't know how they figure to call it tea, it tastes more like pine duff to me." Jack stirred the tea a few times, then put the pot back on the stove to steep.

"I'd love some tea!" Josie handed Jack her cup. "English tea is also my very favorite. I'm afraid Kate has me spoiled!"

"What a coincidence. It was Kate who gave me my first cup of decent tea several years ago when she began to work at the hotel. Before that I don't remember ever having tried the stuff. Miners usually drink coffee when they're not drinking whiskey."

The two continued to talk as the tea was brewing, then a few minutes later Jack said, "It must be ready now, it's been a while." He got up and fetched the pot. Jack poured a steaming cup and passed it across the table to Josie, without letting a drop spill. "I've no saucers but I do have fresh milk and some white sugar." Jack retrieved a milk jug from just outside the back door. Josie assumed there was a root cellar back there somewhere.

Using a long handled ladle he dipped out a bit of the milk and carried it back to the table. Holding the ladle above her cup he asked, "Cream?"

Josie nodded her head with a smile and said, "Yes, please."

After giving both cups a shot of white, he sat down again across from her. He looked at her inquisitively for a moment, and then asked "So how are you liking it here in Buckskin Joe, Miss Pye?"

Josie stirred the sugar in her tea, thinking for a moment, and then said, "Well, I suppose I like it just fine, though I must say it certainly did snow a lot this spring!"

Jack shook his head. "You know, this was a very hard winter, Miss Pye. It's not usually so bad in May and June, but this year we got hit real hard. They say it's one of them hundred year winters. Why I suppose we'll be reading about this in the papers for the rest of our lives!"

He chewed on his lower lip and pondered for a moment. "You know, we are the highest town around here and the weather is rough, even in a regular year. If being warm is your concern then you've come to the worst place in Colorado!"

Josie looked at him as she absorbed this information, and then said, "I see you have quite a collection of books, I love to read myself."

"I ordered those my first winter here, you can buy them by the pound. I have twenty-eight pounds of The Collection of Fine Literature," he said proudly. "You're more than welcome to borrow one anytime, reading sure helps keep me from going crazy with cabin fever in the winter!"

The two of them remained there for some time, drinking their tea and exchanging small talk about the goings on of the town as the golden summer sun sank lower and lower into the dark pine trees above Buckskin Joe. It was the first time since the young horse had died that Jack felt any interest in life again.

As July approached, the snow pack continued to melt at a furious pace. The white snow cover of the mountains gave way to velvety green meadows, and the swollen rivers continued to rise even higher in their banks. In places, the force of the torrent ripped away yards of sand and rock, leaving huge gashes in the reddish brown soil.

One afternoon clouds began to creep over the mountain peaks of the Continental Divide, looking innocent enough as they floated in the sunny blue sky. But anyone who knew anything about summer in those parts would certainly know better.

Afternoon storms were typical fare for a beautiful summer day in the Colorado mountains and most usually accompanied by great displays of thunder and lightning and occasionally hail of varying sizes. The mountain people knew that if they had any work to do outside on a summer day they had better plan to get it done by the noon hour, or it might not get done at all that day.

The few miners-turned-ranchers in the wide open prairie lands of the South Park were up and working before first light each August morning, cutting for the coming winter. Each afternoon when the storms rolled in, these men cursed the rains, which delayed the haying. The hay must lay out for another day in the hot sun to bake totally dry before it could be pitched into the wagon for stacking. Hay stored wet could turn moldy and kill a horse. There was also the possibility it could spontaneously combust from internal heat and start a barn fire.

So the ranchers worried and watched the skies as the hay ripened for cutting. Each afternoon in the fields they raced against the inevitable gathering storm clouds, cutting and stacking furiously as the first patter of raindrops fell on their heads.

A man working the fields never felt rested during haying season. There was never enough time in a good year and never enough rain in a bad year. He was either consumed by worry because of bad weather or working round the clock in good weather until he reached a state of complete exhaustion.

Many a high mountain rancher dreaded the summer haying season more than he did the frigid months of winter when the winds were fierce and relentless, making ranching near to impossible. Yet when they retreated inside their log barns on blizzard days, the hay stacked up to the barn roof was a reminder of the warmth and smell of the summer. Somehow, smelling that sweet, sun-baked hay in the dead of winter seemed to warm a body more quickly than a wood stove might.

The rains held off until the dinner hour, but when they came, they came with a fury. In the steaming pantry Kate looked up from her cooking pots as the first claps of thunder rattled the windowpanes.

"My, that was a close one!" she exclaimed to Tommy, who was helping her peel a small hill of potatoes for the evening meal. "Tommy, you'd best go fetch more dry wood before the rains hit. It's starting already."

The spattering of rain on the tin roof increased rapidly with a force that promised a downpour, unlike the gentle rain that had merely teased the flower blossoms the day before; evaporating rapidly and never reaching the parched roots.

Kate saw the sky was completely darkened with a bank of purple and gray clouds that hung thick and low to the horizon. The last rays of the afternoon sun lit the billowing thunderheads eerily. A huge clap of thunder shook the pots hanging from nails on the wall. Kate bolted upright in her chair. "Mercy! This is going to be a bad one!"

The pantry door was slammed, and Jack Herndon's two dogs slunk in, tails tucked between their legs in fear as they begged to be allowed in from the thunderstorm. Kate looked at their woeful eyes and said, "Oh, I suppose so. Go ahead, you scared dogs. Go on and hide." The dogs headed straight for the parlor and crawled underneath the prickly horsehair sofa. Two sets of eyes peered out from the shadows.

Kate set down her peeling knife and wiped her hands upon her apron. Then she went to the small pantry window and looked out into the rain. Little rivers were already flowing in the ruts of the dirt road. The hard ground was baked so dry that it would not accept the water readily.

Kate held the door open wide for Tommy, who was sodden to the skin. He dumped his load of wood into the box by the stove. She teased him affectionately, "You won't be needing your bath this week Tommy. I'd say you're as clean as you ever get right now!"

Tommy grinned sheepishly at her as she threw her curly head back in laughter.

It was a joke between them, for Kate had to coax Tommy into bathing once a week. When he lived with his drunken father, bathing was a low priority. Perhaps a dunking in a frigid stream might be ventured on a warm summer's day, but to intentionally clean ones' self beyond washing the face and hands was not part of a miner's life. Or at least it had not been part of his father's life, a rough man who stank more from whiskey than his body's own festering smell.

So Tommy found Kate's insistence upon weekly baths in the large tin tub which was filled by many pots of water heated upon the wood stove to be a foreign and unpleasant task. But Kate set the rules. It was her job to run the hotel as she saw fit. When Tommy became so dirty that she noticed, without a word she set out the big tin tub, a clean flower sack for a towel, and a square of white homemade soap beside the stove. Kate would make herself busy in another part of the hotel for a few hours to give Tommy a chance to bathe in privacy. When she returned some time later, she found him scrubbed and fresh smelling, wearing clean clothes, with his thick wet hair hanging like a dripping mop over his eyes.

The lack of civilized bathing accommodations was the one thing that Kate did not like about living in such a rough mining town. Her time to bathe was Sunday evening after dinner, when all the guests had left the kitchen to relax by the wood stove in the parlor or perhaps had wandered off into town.

She tacked a blanket over the doorway for privacy, and tried to bathe as quickly as she could in the shallow water, pouring pitchers of steaming water over her back as she shivered in the drafty kitchen. Then she hopped out and dried herself close to the wood stove before putting on fresh, clean clothes. Whenever she could save enough money, Kate's one indulgence was to take the stage over Hoosier Pass to Breckenridge and stay at the Brown Hotel for a night, specifically to use it's bathtub. People traveled for miles just to indulge in the delicious warmth of the steaming tub. It was the only place to properly bathe short of Denver.

Kate's money jar had a ways to go before the level of coins was high enough for her to afford her next night's stay and a luxurious bath. She treasured those trips to Breckenridge, the thriving mining town that lay along the gold-rich Blue River that flowed down the opposite side of the Continental Divide from Buckskin Joe.

Breckenridge was close to Buckskin Joe in size, yet had a different type of life that made a refreshing change for Kate each time she traveled there. There were better stores where Kate could purchase such items as fabric, thread, and spices. It was just plain fun to get out of Buckskin Joe for a few nights and escape from the daily duties of the hotel kitchen while leaving Jack and Tommy in charge. Kate loved to stroll along the streets of Breckenridge while admiring the breathtaking views of the mountain peaks tipped in snow that seemed close enough to touch and to see the lovely flower gardens of the fine houses in town.

In Buckskin Joe the thick pine forest grew close to the streets of town and obscured the view of the Mosquito Mountains in most places. The view in Breckenridge was so open that it made one feel higher up and closer to the sky. Something in Kate's soul always felt so free and light as she gazed out across the Ten Mile Range in Breckenridge, far above any obscuring forests.

Feeling relaxed and fresh after a long, soaking bath Kate would sit by the window in her room at the Brown Hotel, and with the weather willing she would let the bright mountain sun dry her thick brown hair into its natural screw curls as she lightly rubbed it with a soft towel. Then, feeling her very best she would put on one of her finest dresses that was saved for special occasions. She took great pains to pin her hair up in the latest fashion beneath her fancy hat before ascending the hotel staircase to stroll along the streets of Breckenridge. She felt quite the lady.

She stopped when the urge struck her, here and there to purchase some small items and enjoying poking around the shops as much as she did walking about the picturesque streets of the town. She felt as if she were the queen of England herself; what a luxury it was to not think of preparing the hotel's meals, cooking over the steaming pots and piles of greasy dishes to attend to. It was pure bliss!

Admittedly, Kate did sometimes let her mind wander back to Buckskin Joe at meal times, and she would wonder how Jack and Tommy were fairing. But she quickly forced these thoughts from her mind for she knew she would all too soon return to the poorly swept kitchen with food bits beneath the chairs and burned pots cluttering the countertop in her kitchen.

Try as she might to teach Tommy how to cook a simple meal or two, the boy seemed destined to ruin most of the meals he prepared alone. He could never remember to check the stews and soups before they had burned fast to the bottom of the pot, imparting a terrible scorched flavor to the entire meal.

The lack of income during these times did not bother Kate, for she knew ahead of time that the only customers for the kitchen would be the stagecoach passengers who were none the wiser, being there for only their overnight stay.

As the rain continued to beat furiously on the roof, the clock chimed four o'clock. "Heavens!" exclaimed Kate, "Look at the time!" After requesting Tommy's help, Kate then flew into a flurry of activity which none could match, and in a short time she had set the table with pans of delicious golden brown fried potatoes and onions, plates of tender baked elk steaks, several baskets of fresh bakery rolls, small plates of white cream butter, and pitchers of gravy.

Everything was ready just in time, for the scraping of boots upon the porch could be heard not one minute after the last pan of fried potatoes was set on the table.

As the heavy door swung open, Kate looked up to see who was coming in first, and her heart leaped when she saw Samuel Grey

He tipped his hat to her, then said, "Good day, Miss Kate."

She broke into a peal of laughter, as a stream of water from his hat brim poured onto the floor.

"Why, hello Samuel!" she replied merrily, "How was your drive today? Or was it more of a swim?" Samuel grinned back at her. He extended his wet hand as he stepped closer to her. "You look fetching, Kate. That's a right nice dress you have on. I've been thinking of you." She let him take her hand, and she felt like she was floating.

His strong calloused hand enveloped hers. "I hope I may have some more of your company this evening. There is something I would like to show you," Samuel said.

With her cheeks flushed hot with pleasure, Kate finally withdrew her hand from his and replied, "That would be fine, Samuel. I'm sure Tommy will lend a hand in clearing up dinner. Say about seven o'clock?" She smiled back at him as the stage passengers began to fill the low-ceilinged parlor with their laughter, as they removed their rain soaked coats and laid them to dry by the fire.

Samuel took a few steps back to the door and again tipped his hat. "At seven, then!" and he was gone out the door to attend to his wet and tired team, leaving Kate to feed her dinner guests.

All through that meal Kate's mind was elsewhere, and she served food and poured drinks for the grateful group automatically. Her mind rambled ahead to the upcoming evening with Samuel. She could still feel the pressure of his hand and the intensity of his eyes. Her heart skipped a beat in anticipation.

Even though she was excited, she felt somehow strangely calm. "Life's a river and I'm a leaf upon it," she whispered to herself, aware that she was letting herself be swept away so pleasantly by a force much greater than her own.

As the evening meal drew to a close Kate kept an eye on the black hands of the small clock that stood on the mantle. She had in mind a quick escape from the kitchen and was determined to have a few minutes to attend to her appearance before meeting Samuel. After sweetening Tommy to the idea of cleaning the dinner mess alone, Kate untied her apron and made a hasty exit from the cluttered kitchen. It was ten minutes to seven.

Kate splashed water into her washing basin and washed her face. By two minutes to seven, with her hair freshly combed and pinned and wearing her second best dress, Kate descended the hotel staircase. She wasn't kept waiting—Samuel was already knocking on the door as she reached the parlor.

She opened the heavy wooden door and was greeted by a beaming Samuel whose hair was plastered to his head and smelled of rum after-shave. He was holding a small bouquet of wildflowers—bluebells, columbine, and purple aspen daisies. He extended the flowers and said, "I hope you like flowers, Kate."

She took the bouquet from him and breathed deeply of their sweet scent. "Mmmm. These are beautiful! Thank you, Samuel. Come on back to the kitchen with me, and I'll find a jar to put them in."

He followed her through the swinging half doors. The counters were still piled high with dirty dishes. Kate selected a mason jar from the small pantry's highest shelf, then dipped it in the covered water bucket to fill it. She set the jar of flowers on the windowsill above the sink.

"There! Now I can enjoy them when I am working in the kitchen, and," Kate fluttered her eyelashes at Samuel, "they will make me think of you."

His kiss was full of passion, and she felt an answering pang awake within her. As she felt his strong arms encircle her and she felt the stubble of his beard against her cheek, she wondered if this man was to be a big part of her future. Samuel put his hand into his coat pocket and took out a tightly folded handkerchief tied with a thin piece of string. He held it out to her and said, "This is for you, Kate. Open it."

She glanced at him curiously and said, "For me? Why, what could it be?" She untied the small piece of white string and carefully unrolled the cloth. Inside lay a small golden ring set with three green stones.

Samuel picked up the ring and said, "It was my mother's ring and her mother's before that. I'd like for you to have it, Kate. See if it fits."

Kate's hand trembled slightly as she tried it on several fingers before finding one that was small enough. She laughed as she said, "My family always was known for their big bones! I am lucky, it just fits my smallest finger." She looked down at ring, the green stones sparkling against the gold. "It's beautiful, Samuel. I've never seen such a lovely ring. How could I possible accept it?"

Samuel smiled at her and said, "We can go to a jeweler in Denver and have it enlarged, to fit your ring finger."

He took her face between his two large hands. Before she could open her lips to answer him he kissed her again, right there in the kitchen surrounded by piles of dirty dishes.

When he drew his face back from hers, she smiled up at him and said softly, "I'll treasure it always, Samuel. I'll never take it off."

FOUR

JUST AS SUMMER DECLINED and the new coolness began changing deep green aspen leaves to their brilliant autumn yellow, winter arrived. On a late September morning, Jack Herndon awoke to a cold, gray light coming through his cabin window. He peered out and to his dismay saw the corral and barn covered in several inches of pristine snow. Nipper thumped his tail joyfully when he heard his master stirring and leaped up to the edge of the loft bed, resting his front paws against the mattress.

Jack stroked the thickening fur and sighed. "Nipper, why did it have to snow already? It's just too early!" He sighed again, thinking of the chores he must rise and get to, chores that had been far more pleasant in the sunny, crisp Indian summer days than they would be now.

It saddened him to think that snow had come before the full turning of the aspens. It was such a beautiful time of year when the forests blazed golden beneath the bright blue skies. In fact, it was his favorite time of year.

Today the sky itself seemed depressed; it was a dull gray color and looked a little dirty against the fresh, white landscape. Somehow the gloom made a snowy morning much more of an injustice.

Just a stone's throw down the hill from Jack's cabin, in one of the upstairs private rooms of the hotel, Josie lay in bed, feeling little motivation to rise on the chilly, dreary morning. She could see the snow-covered pines from her high window and remembered that in St. Louis it never snowed so early. It was much nearer to Christmas that white flakes would cover the grimy, crowded city. As a child she thought everything looked clean and magical.

Under the heavy warm quilts, her thoughts took her to the recent past and Horace. "Now stop that!" she scolded herself. One thing living in Buckskin Joe taught her—no matter what the weather, you got on with life.

But there were times, such as now, when a memory from the past was sparked and Josie could not keep herself from remembering when she had been in love—how wonderful it had been and how swiftly and painfully it had ended.

The memory of Horace sent a pain through her chest. Hot tears formed pools in her ears as she watched the ceiling blur.

She closed her eyes and spoke sternly to herself, but the tears flowed even stronger. When would she get over Horace? She lay curled on her side in defeat, and clasped her pillow tightly as she wept into it, attempting to stifle the noise from her sobbing.

How betrayed and lost she had felt from the moment she saw him and his family! All the tender words he had spoken to her which she had believed rang like tinny lies in her head. How utterly young and foolish she'd been to let herself be swayed by sweet words, to give her virtue to a man who cared not a straw for her.

Downstairs in the kitchen Kate sat in her chair by the warm stove, stroking the striped gray cat, Henry, who was curled in her lap. The potatoes were frying in the skillet, and the first pot of coffee was on to boil. The gray sky and snowy landscape outside dampened her usual cheery mood.

A strange noise came from upstairs, it sounded like the whining of a distressed cat. Henry woke from his slumber with a start, digging his claws into Kate's legs.

"Ouch!" she exclaimed, unceremoniously dumping the cat from her lap.

She heard the noise again, and recognized the sound of crying. It was Josie.

Kate went upstairs and knocked on Josie's door. "Josie, are you all right? May I come in?"

"Yes, come in," said Josie.

Kate stepped into the narrow room. It was dreary and chilly, without the usual bright sunshine streaming through the window. Josie hoisted herself up on her elbows, clutching the quilts about her. Kate noticed her red, swollen eyes, and the tell tale tracks of wet lingering on her cheeks.

"I thought I heard you crying, are you ill?" Kate asked with concern. "Shall I fetch Dr. Matson?"

Josie managed a wan smile.

"I'll be alright, thank you for checking on me, Kate." She pushed her unkempt hair from her face and accepted the handkerchief that Kate handed her. She blew her nose and continued.

"What's wrong with me, no Doctor can fix. Unless they've invented a cure for love..." Josie laughed. "Who ever discovers that will be rich, won't they!" She looked at Kate seriously and said "Kate, I'll get dressed and come down. It's as good a time as any to tell you what happened before I came to Buckskin Joe. Maybe it will help if I get it off my chest."

When Josie came into the kitchen Kate set a plate of biscuits and jam in front of her. "The coffee's almost ready, would you like a cup?"

"Yes, please," answered Josie, as she took a seat. She looked at Kate for a moment before beginning her story.

"I've never told anyone this before Kate, but I know you'll keep this in your confidence."

Kate nodded her head in acknowledgement, and Josie continued.

"I came here from St. Louis to get away from a man. I met Horace at my mother's seamstress shop. What a handsome man he was! I will never forget the first day I saw him." The memory flooded her with emotion, but it was a relief to talk about it.

"Horace was the first man I ever loved, and I believed everything he told me. It never occurred that he would lie to me, he didn't seem like the kind of man who would." Her eyes narrowed and she said, "Horace told me he traveled on business purchasing for his company, and he came to St. Louis frequently. We met every time he came, usually once a week."

Kate rose from the table to get the coffee pot. "How did you find out he was lying?" she asked curiously.

"We had been seeing each other for almost six months. He would send a note to the shop and I would meet him at his hotel. He kept a room there." She laughed spitefully and said, "And that was a lie too, I'm sure! He probably lived in Saint Louis all along!"

Josie looked up from the biscuit she was idly tearing into small pieces upon her plate. "I saw him on market day in the city. He was with his wife and two boys."

"Are you sure it was his wife, Josie? Perhaps it was his sister?" Kate ventured.

"No, I am certain of it. I heard them talking. It was his wife and children," said Josie.

"Did he see you?" asked Kate.

Josie grit her teeth before answering in a voice tight with anger. "Yes, he saw me alright! Then he turned his back to me and walked away. That was the last time I ever saw him. I left St. Louis the next morning on the train. I couldn't stand to see him, or even think about him. I needed to get away, far away!"

"So do you still care for him, even after what he did?" asked Kate. "Is that why you were crying?"

Josie sat quietly for a moment, her brow furrowed in thought.

"Yes, I still care for him. I know he misled me and I should hate him for that, but I can't. Falling out of love isn't an easy thing. I just can't stop thinking about him," said Josie.

Kate leaned across the table towards Josie. "It hasn't been that long yet. I'm sure with time you'll be able to leave it behind you," she said hopefully. "When my last beau left to go to California I was miserable for a while, but then one day I realized I had forgotten to think about him. After that it just got easier." She grasped Josie's hand. "You'll see, Josie. Soon you won't even think of him at all."

Josie lifted her still swollen eyes to Kate's. "I hope you're right Kate, for I can't stand too many more mornings like today. I hate to cry about it. It gives me the worst headache and I feel awful all day afterwards."

"That's normal, Josie. That's just the way I felt. Why don't you take the morning off and go have some time for yourself, I can handle the kitchen just fine."

Josie smiled at her friend. "You're good to me Kate. It helped to talk to you, I feel better now. Maybe I'll go down to the mercantile and buy some material for a dress. I've wanted to do some sewing. Are you sure you don't want me to stay through breakfast?"

Kate shooed her out, waving her hands in the air. "Nonsense! You go on, I'll be just fine, there's barely anyone in town now anyhow!"

Josie went back upstairs to her room feeling immensely improved in spirits and prepared herself for this impromptu outing.

Outside the high kitchen window, the slow drizzled began to turn to snow. Rain and snow hissed in the chimney, and the fire popped and snapped inside the large cast iron cooking stove. The front door opened, letting in a sudden gust of cold air. Jack came in quickly and closed the door against the weather, then tipped his hat at Kate.

"Morning, Kate. Mind if I sit down and warm up?" he asked.

"Not at all, you can be company for me when I finish getting breakfast ready. It's almost done, help yourself to coffee while I fry the eggs." She rapidly cracked open the eggs one by one and dropped them into the skillet of hot grease. "There! It's fried potatoes, eggs, and biscuits this morning."

Jack pulled a chair up to the table and sat down across from Kate. "I sure did enjoy that dinner you had Josie bring over to me, Kate. You make the best stew I ever had." Kate accepted the compliment with a slight nod of her head. Jack looked down at his work worn hands as he continued.

"Just haven't been able to get myself a decent meal since Buddy died. I guess I haven't really cared enough to know what I'm eating." He shook his head. "You just never know what's going to happen—here I was set to find the old horse dead any day, then it's the two year old who dies!"

Kate reached out and gently touched Jack's arm. "Buddy was a beautiful horse, I miss him too. Every time I make stew I think of him. I used to save the carrot ends for him."

"Yeah, he always had a funny side. Never knew a horse like that. I remember one day when he unrolled twenty feet of roofing paper I left too close to the corral, just for the heck of it, and chewed holes through the whole thing. And he used to steal nails from my can when I was fixing fence. He'd just take them up in his mouth for a bit then spit them out."

"You shouldn't fret about him Jack, he lived a good life. He was a lucky animal to have you as an owner. He never knew a hungry day or the mean end of a whip."

"Thank you, Kate. I appreciate your kind words. You're a good woman."

Kate bit her lip in a moment of deep thought. Then she looked up at Jack and said, "There is something I'd like to ask your help with, Jack. It's Josie. I'm worried about her. She's been looking poorly lately, and I'm at my wits end as to what to do. Perhaps if you were to ask her out for an outing it would lift her spirits. Would you do that as a favor to me, Jack?"

Jack perked up at the mention of Josie's name. He mulled over the idea of asking Josie for an outing. He liked the idea. "Kate, if you think that it would be of help to Josie, it would be a pleasure. Perhaps you would tell her that I would be honored by her company for a ride after dinner on Friday evening. I'll be here at seven." Jack stood up. "Well, I best be getting to my chores."

Kate noticed a spring in Jack's step as he shut the back door. She remained seated alone as the gathering darkness of the storm set in and stole the colors gradually from the room. Through the window she watched the blowing aspen branches that created shadowy patterns across the wall.

It had been an unusually draining day, and for a rare change Kate had abandoned her regular routine. She felt the strangeness of all this thinking and sensed the heaviness of the emotions that were controlling the lives of those friends she felt most strongly about. Then Kate, always the pillar of strength and dependability for the people around her lay her forehead against her hands and prayed. She felt her friend's pain as if it were her own. If there was any way she could make things better she would—but maybe God could help.

The next morning the sun shone down warmly upon the grassy hillside surrounding Buckskin Joe as if it were a summer day. Jack woke early on this day, and threw the quilt off him. On such a splendid day Jack could not help feeling happy, not just because of the woodsy scents of autumn floating on the warm October sunshine. Today, he would see Josie!

Since Kate had asked him to invite Josie for an outing, the worlds' colors had brightened and his heart had begun to sing with the birds that nested in the nearby pines. Gone was his former ill-at-ease with her. Perhaps Buddy's death brought into sharp focus how short life was. Still he wondered if fate hadn't taken matters out of his hands. Would he have ever had the courage to ask Josie out? No matter. It was all arranged.

As Jack dressed in the chill air of the cabin and got ready to do his morning chores excitement mounted with each hour. He stepped out into the first slanting rays of sunshine coming in stripes through the woods and felt the warmth on his body. The dogs leaped and ran in circles about him as they headed up toward the barn to feed the mare and cows. The blood was moving in his limbs and he breathed deeply. Was life always so wonderful?

That evening at seven o'clock Jack arrived at the hotel steps with his bay mare and a dapple gray gelding borrowed from the Jenkins. He tied the two handsome horses to the hitching post and prepared to call on Josie. Jack didn't have a "good" suit, but he'd taken great pains to clean and press his denim pants and brown woolen shirt. He was freshly bathed, and the buttons on his shirt cuffs had been fastened beneath his coat. His face was shaved smooth and his hair combed. Although he was somewhat nervous, there was a strong, confident air about him as he strode up the wide steps of the hotel porch.

Josie sat just inside the door, on the prickly green horsehair sofa. She clenched her black-gloved fingers in her lap as she waited. She was dressed in Kate's borrowed riding clothes. The two of them had spent the afternoon taking in several inches on the skirt, for it had hung on Josie's slight frame. Between the pins held in Kate's mouth she clucked about Josie not eating enough. Once altered, her outfit accented her slim waist and round hips. It wasn't her looks that had Josie nervous. It was her riding abilities.

She had very hazy memories of being led around a field of deep yellow grass on a cart horse at her grandfather's farm back in Missouri. She couldn't have been older than seven or eight years old, because shortly after her grandfather died the farm was sold. As she recalled, she'd not let go of her grandfather's hand the whole time.

When Jack opened the door and saw Josie looking up at him his heart leaped beneath his coat. "What a fine evening Miss Pye. Are you ready to go for a ride? We still have an hour of good light left." He extended his hand to the pretty woman. There were spots of color high on her pale cheeks, and she seemed a bit flustered as she gathered the heavy woolen riding skirt about her.

She caught her breath for a moment as she grasped the hand he offered to help her down the stairs. It was strange, she thought to herself, that she had never before noticed what a nice looking man Jack was.

"I am not a very practiced rider, Mr. Herndon. I hope the horse I will be riding is gentle."

He tried not to stare at her striking beauty, "Why, you needn't worry. All the children get their first lessons on Old Storm. Why, even the babies ride him round the barn with just a piece of twine for reins. We'll both take good care of you.

Relieved at his words, Josie glanced at him before going down the porch stairs to the waiting horses. Now that she could put her worries aside, she frankly examined the man as he untied the team. She decided she liked his square jaw, somber blue eyes and wide mouth with the brown mustache that fit him so well. He's always so quiet you'd miss him if you weren't looking for him, she thought. Still, Jack seemed intelligent and perceptive which only added to the attraction. Perhaps she had never thought of it because he always seemed to be in the background of the noisier crowds of miners that flooded the town's establishments and streets.

Suddenly she realized she was attracted to him. Jack Herndon seemed different. There was something so plain and natural about his looks, so unlike the men she had known in St. Louis. He didn't need a fancy hat or expensive clothes. As Jack grasped her hand to help her mount Old Storm Josie detected the faintest whiff of soap. He must have just recently bathed. She approved.

Jack was such a different kind of man. He looked so naturally a part of the mountains. She couldn't imagine him living in any other environment; certainly not the city streets of St. Louis! He seemed a part of the mountains of Colorado just as the plants and wild creatures did. She'd noticed in the past that he made no attempt toward pretensions to impress people. He was who he was, and she agreed with Kate—he was a very handsome man.

Jack easily mounted his bay mare and led the way up Buckskin Joe toward the mountains and the forest.

After an uneventful ride evening set in, and it became chillier. The sun still shone above the mountains, and the late September evening couldn't have been lovelier for a ride. By the time they reached Kite Lake the sun was about to slip behind the steep rocky peaks. Jack helped Josie off her horse and then tied both the horses to a buffalo berry bush. Josie looked at the lake and the close, high peaks that formed a bowl marking the end of the valley. The sheer, steep slopes were truly impressive. Just five miles away in Buckskin Joe the mountains seemed remote, but standing here immediately beneath them she could clearly see the rock fields and sand slides all the way to the summit.

Two fat picas stood on their hind legs atop a large boulder, showing their furry, honey colored bellies. They emitted strange, high-pitched calls, and Josie had learned this meant danger. There were many things Josie had discovered about this new country since she came to live in Buckskin Joe.

Jack unrolled the woolen blanket tied behind his saddle for emergencies. Under the last bit of sunlight, they sat upon the blanket and watched the fish surfacing to eat flies, creating radiating patterns on the golden surface of the water. Shadows were deepening in the mountains and Josie shivered. The silence was companionable.

Jack knew that there would never be a better time to get to know Josie. He must make an overture now.

"I'm glad you came up here with me Josie. It's been too long since I've gotten away from town. There's always plenty of work for me to do at the hotel and saloon."

"Owning the place must keep you busy, do you like it?" asked Josie.

"I like it better than mining, but I can't say I want to do this for the rest of my life," said Jack. "I built the hotel the spring after the big strike. That's when people really started coming here. It was a good time to start the business, and I can't complain. I built the saloon in the fall. The only thing I don't like is having to deal with people—especially when they're drunk! It gets tiring. I guess that's why I spend so much time messing around the barn with the horses. It gets me away from the people." He picked a thick stalk of grass and chewed it, sucking out the sweet juice.

Jack could scarcely believe that Josie was sitting beside him. This was just what he had hoped for, a chance to be alone with this beautiful woman. Just as he was shifting closer to Josie, to be close enough to touch her, she spoke again.

"What would you do if you sold the hotel, Jack? Go back to mining?"

"No, what I'd like to do is get some ranch land before it's all settled up out here. My family had a farm back in New York. We grew feed corn and raised hogs. I'd like to get land down south where it's warm enough to raise crops. It's real nice along the Arkansas river," he said.

Jack was now positioned close enough to Josie that his arm brushed against hers. He was sure that Josie must sense his desire for her, which seemed impossible to contain.

"I've never lived on a farm, but when I was a girl we'd go to my grandparents place out in the country. We'd stay for weeks. There was a big garden; we picked buckets of tomatoes and beans. Grandma canned enough for the winter; the cellar was full to the ceiling with jars. In the fall we picked apples and pressed cider. That was our favorite." Josie smoothed her skirt over her knees. "When Grandpa died the farm was sold and Grandma came to live in St. Louis with my Aunt. I missed going out to the farm, I was still a little girl then. The country is such fun when you're a child." Josie fell silent, thinking back to those childhood years at the farm.

Jack nodded in agreement. "When I have children I want to be on a ranch, not in town. There's time enough later to learn about cities and people. It's important to learn about raising food and living in nature when you're young. Then it gets in your blood and you never forget it."

Jack put his hand on top of Josie's. She turned her palm upward, accepting his touch and allowing their fingers to entwine.

When the last rays had vanished from the sky, Jack stood up and helped Josie to her feet. She was glad she only came to his chest, because she was afraid if he could see her eyes, he'd see her interest. And what if their relationship ended the way it did with Horace? She couldn't let that happen.

They finally mounted up and rode back toward Buckskin Joe, a silver sliver of moon rising behind them. Somehow they both knew something wonderful had begun. Old Storm followed placidly along behind the bay mare, and Josie watched Jack's strong back proceeding down the road in front of her. Being with him made her feel secure and safe.

When they arrived at the hotel, Jack swung off his horse and helped Josie dismount from the gray. She held tightly as she awkwardly swung her leg over the saddle horn. The heavy riding skirt made it difficult. Once she was on the ground Jack held her for a moment.

"I sure do thank you for coming with me tonight, Josie. Perhaps you'd come again for another ride, tomorrow night?"

Josie's heart lurched as she tried not to gush with enthusiasm. "I'd like nothing better, Jack! That is, if Old Storm will let me ride him again." She stroked the horse's neck, which smelled of horse sweat, a distinctive scent she was beginning to like. "He was a good horse to put up with me!"

Jack's face lit up. "We'll come pick you up. Same time?"

Josie nodded. "You coming to breakfast, Jack?"

"Wouldn't miss it for the world, Goodnight Josie!"

Josie stood in the darkness and watched Jack disappear. She breathed deeply of the cool night air and noticed how bright and close the stars seemed that night. After a minute or two, she gathered her skirt and went up the wide wooden steps of the porch and into the hotel.

FIVE

As October turned to November, the last days of Indian summer gave way to winter. One night, the winds howled and shrieked through the treetops, threatening to rip them from the ground. Yet when the sun cast its first rays over the frozen land, both the trees and the rooftops remained intact.

Far out on the edge of the Great South Park, in the freezing morning air, Samuel Grey sat on the driver's seat of the stage under several thick woolen blankets. A scarf obscured all but his eyes and his hat was pulled low down over his ears. No snow lay on the ground, but the freezing winds were enough to give a person frostbite.

Winter frostbite or summer mosquito bite, Samuel liked his job. He was glad for this solitary time away from the chatter of the passengers. It wasn't that he didn't like people; it was just that when he drove the stage through the plains of the South Park he preferred the company of the birds, the wild animals, and the winds. His favorite leg of the journey began where the dirt road crossed over Kenosha Pass and he saw the breathtaking expanse of the South Park. Contained by a ring of mountains, the flat grasslands stretched over fifty miles. The distant peaks rose out of the haze in varied shades of blue and mauve, reminding Samuel of the ocean which he had seen several times as a boy growing up in the east.

If any one place described the West, it was here. Traveling through this section of the high mountains with their wild beauty lifted Samuel's spirits.

Samuel liked to keep moving. There was something in him that rebelled against settling and staying put in one place. He felt his soul would gather dust, as does an unopened book on a table. When asked if he missed having a home to call his own, Samuel replied, "I like to travel." Each new day brought new situations and little that was routine.

As the stage approached Buckskin Joe in the early morning breeze Samuel became excited. The thought of Kate's company was intoxicating. For the past months they had spent a lot of time together. The separations were hard to bear and they treasured what little time they had together.

Although it was almost an hour early when Samuel pulled the steaming team to a halt in front of the hotel, Kate burst from the front door, still wearing her kitchen apron, greeting him with a hug. It was hard for her to concentrate as she directed the passengers into the dining room and served the first round of coffee. Finally, she pulled Samuel into the pantry and flung her arms around his strong neck and covered his wind-burned and bristly face with kisses.

"Samuel, I have missed you! I'm so glad you are here!" She clung tightly to him and buried her face in his neck.

Samuel kissed the top of her curly brown head. "I missed you too, Kate." It felt good to hold Kate again.

When she lifted her tousled head from his shoulder he said, "Come with me Kate, while I put the team up in the barn. And get yourself a coat. Don't want my sweetheart to catch her death!" Kate obeyed and then with Samuels' arm settled comfortably about her shoulders, they headed for the barn.

For one night a week the two shared a joy neither had known before. Perhaps it was the limited time together that made their attraction so strong. After all, both had slept with other people before, but the passion had never been like this

෫

THERE WAS, HOWEVER, one memory that haunted Samuel at times. It involved a woman. A year or two before Kate had come to run the hotel kitchen at Buckskin Joe, a young woman named Georgina worked at the large yellow sporting house on the hill in Alma. As best he could remember she wasn't exactly beautiful, but she had an attractive figure.

Considering the rough country, a man was lucky to find even a mildly attractive woman. This wasn't Boston or St. Louis, after all. Few women, even whores, wanted to spend a winter freezing in the high mountain mining camps of Colorado. Given the lack of competition, Georgina had a steady stream of males wishing to engage her services.

When Samuel thought of her he felt ashamed, and remembered how little she had meant to him as a person. Few words had ever passed between them. Then one spring morning right before sunrise, just about eight hours after Samuel had been with her Georgina hung herself with a bed sheet from the balcony of the yellow house.

It was a painful memory that Samuel could not erase from his mind. He wondered if he had contributed to her reason for hanging herself. He remembered her frightened, panicky eyes, which had reminded him of the eyes of a cornered rabbit.

After Samuel pulled all the hay from Kate's hair, and buckled his pants, they parted from their hasty encounter with a passionate kiss. Kate headed for the kitchen and Samuel to the bakery. They both knew he'd join her in her bedroom that night.

By midmorning, Samuel had drunk his second cup of coffee. He studied the growing cloudbank over Hoosier Pass. The heavy wooden sign hanging from iron rings thumped and banged loudly against the storefront as the wind picked up. The bright sunlight shining through the small panes of wavy glass did not fool Samuel.

"Looks like we're in for some weather today, Tim."

The baker, who was busy mixing a large bowl of bread dough, nodded. "Sure enough does, Samuel. Mosquito Pass was socked in at sunrise. Coming into town this morning, you couldn't even see the peak of Tip-Top Mountain. Must be blowing like all hell up there. Hope this change in weather doesn't mess up the dough I have rising. Sometimes a big storm does, and I have a big baking going today. Nothin' worse than bread that don't rise right."

Tim finished mixing up his dough. He covered the bowl with a clean flour sack, and then sprinkled some water drops onto the cloth before he set it to rise on a high shelf where the air was warm from the ovens. He wiped his hands on his floury apron and came over with the metal coffee pot and an empty cup.

"Mind my company for a minute Samuel? I'm ready for a sit down, been up most the night."

Samuel pulled a chair out from the table for his friend. "My pleasure, Tim. Set a spell with me."

He took a sip from the hot coffee, and then leaned back in his chair and stretched his flour-speckled legs in front of him. "Ahhh. Soon as Chris gets in, I'm goin' home to bed. Got to get some rest before I go up to the house and see the ladies. Don't want to waste my money fallin' asleep with 'em!"

After yawning mightily, he began to read the week-old Fairplay paper. Buckskin Joe didn't put out a newspaper, so the Fairplay *Flume* was where the townspeople found out what was going on in the rest of the world.

By the time Samuel drained his third cup of coffee, the bakery door opened and Chris, Tim's partner, came in. He was accompanied by a great gust of cold wind.

"Mornin', boys!" said the tall, nearly bald Chris. "That wind sure is feisty. Better hold onto your hats good and tight when you go out. It even blew my water trough over; that's one heavy trough, too." He pulled up another chair and brought a cup over to the table. "Got an extra cup in that pot for me?"

They sat in companionable silence, each to their own thoughts. The heavy wooden sign outside continued to bang, the windows rattled, the bread rose. After his fifth cup of coffee Samuel finally came to a decision. He stood up from the table and put on his coat and hat.

"Stage isn't going to run today", he said. "Can't risk a breakdown in this weather. I'd best get over to the hotel and let the passengers know. Thanks for the coffee." He tipped his large hat brim at the two men.

❦

That night snow did fall. In the morning Kate hated to leave the warm bed and Samuel's body, but the stranded passengers would need their breakfast.

The tall yellow prairie grass seemed to glow where it rose above the clean white snow. Beside the soft white banks of the creek bed, the willow shoots, now bare of leaves, shone a brilliant shade of red. In the streets and yards of town the laughter of young children rang out through the cold winter afternoon as the season's first crop of snowmen sprang to life. As dusk fell, the tired but happy children disappeared into their homes to eat their dinners and hang their sodden clothes by the hot wood stoves. The snowmen guarded the night.

Under the cover of darkness a herd of pronghorn became bold and ventured lower down the mountain to graze in a field on the outskirts of town. In just one day the country had changed from autumn to winter. That evening Buckskin Joe was as lovely and festive as a winter painting, with smoke curling from chimneys against the bluish white, snow-covered forest.

Inside the hotel, stranded stage passengers relaxed after dinner in front of the wood stove in the parlor, sipping hot grog. Kate had set a large cast iron pot on top of the stove, and the fragrance of the wine, cinnamon and cloves filled the room. A basket of golden brown sugar cookies lay on the sideboard, next to a stack of cups and saucers. The snowfall outside made the atmosphere inside rather festive, and the guests chattered amongst themselves as though they had known each other for years.

Kate and Josie talked about the upcoming Christmas party.

"It's the biggest night of the year in Buckskin Joe. First there's the dance down at the schoolhouse, then we have dinner here at the hotel. Everyone brings food for the dinner so we don't have to cook it all. And

Saint Nicholas comes, and we open the presents. The party goes on all night, you'll just love it Josie!"

"I can't wait; think of how excited all the children will be!" said Josie.

"You can help me decorate the hotel, we'll tie pine boughs and ribbon around the doors and up the stairway. And Jack always cuts a big spruce for the Christmas tree. We light the candles on the tree for the party." She turned and gave Samuel a quick kiss and squeezed his hand. "And this year will be the best, because my sweetheart will be here with me on Christmas!" said Kate.

Josie glanced across the room at Jack. Who knows, perhaps she too might have a man to call her own for the Christmas party.

Many families in Buckskin Joe barely had enough money to get by in a regular month. As the winter holidays approached, they put thought and time toward creating gifts for friends and relatives, especially for the children. Josie had turned her thoughts toward the coming holidays and kept herself busy sewing little striped red and white flannel stockings for each of the town's children. She planned to fill them with hard sugar candy and hang them up for the hotel's Christmas Eve party.

The next morning, while the passengers ate breakfast inside the hotel, Samuel reluctantly prepared the team to leave Buckskin Joe. It had certainly been a wonderful time for everyone, to have been stranded an additional night at the hotel. The passengers had been made as welcome as old friends during their unexpected stay in Buckskin Joe.

Most times Samuel enjoyed the company of loved ones and the warm fireside, but he wondered if the call of the open road on the stagecoach would ever cease for him. The pain he felt as he left Kate behind was sharp, but his need for freedom was strong. As he grew closer to Kate, this internal battle intensified. He knew he couldn't have them both.

Kate stood at the railing of the porch and watched the stage roll slowly out of town over the new snow, leaving two straight lines of wheel tracks behind it. Tears rolled down her cheeks as she watched the stage grow smaller and smaller, until it vanished into nothingness against the white snow-covered hills to the north.

Josie stood next to her friend, wrapped in her shawl in the biting wind. "Kate, don't be so sad," she begged her friend as she held onto her arm.

"Josie, it's just harder for me every time he leaves. It was so nice to have him for two whole nights. I found myself longing for Samuel to stay. I think I love him."

Josie put her arm around Kate's shoulders, and led her inside the hotel.

"You're going to be so happy next week when Samuel comes back. Why you'll never know you missed him at all! It was you yourself who told me that the two of you get on so well because you have that time apart." Josie chattered brightly about light matters as she prepared a pot a tea. "Kate, let's sit. It's been such a long time since we've had tea together."

Kate seemed content to be waited upon, and sat quietly in her favorite wooden chair beside the cook stove as she looked out the window toward the mountain pass. She knew that right at this moment Samuel was out there somewhere, driving his team of bays across the snowy land, going farther away from her as each moment passed. Having just been here so recently with her, in this very kitchen eating a healthy portion of fried potatoes, gravy, and biscuits, his presence lingered. She wondered if he was thinking of her at this moment or if he had turned his mind forward toward his upcoming journey.

As the tea water began to hiss and boil in the pot, Kate said, "Josie, I suppose this is what love is. I feel as if a part of me has gone away with him too. And it hurts, even though I'd rather have him some than not at all. She sighed. "It just doesn't make any sense, does it?"

Kate managed a wry smile as Josie poured the boiling water into the kettle and added several spoonfuls of loose black tea.

Josie pursed her lips thoughtfully and said, "You know Kate, love is a strange and confusing thing. At times, love hurt me so much that I would rather have been dead than deal with the pain. I'm so glad I didn't die. Just before I came to Colorado I never thought I would ever be able to feel love for a man again. I was running as fast as I could away from it, for I truly felt that it would kill me to stay near the man I could not have for my own." She looked down at the table and ran her finger along the edge of the white cloth that covered it. "This was after I found out that he was married, and had a family. I didn't know that when I first met him; he kept it from me for some time." She looked up again, and met Kate's gaze. "But that's behind me, and I have Jack to think about now. I suppose that love is a thing that travels on to new towns and new lives with different people. But it's a powerful and strange thing. That I truly believe."

The two women sat in the warm kitchen and continued to talk as only good friends can. After several cups of tea, Kate rose from her chair.

"Well, I suppose I'd best get started on the chores. This hotel won't run itself, will it? Thank you for making the tea Josie, and for talking with me. I feel better now."

Josie smiled back at her friend before leaving the kitchen to go upstairs to her room to do a bit of sewing.

Though Kate said these words and meant them too, the sadness of Samuel's departure stayed with her throughout the day like a cloud. As she went about her chores she revisited memories of the past two days—the sound of Samuel's laughter, the shine in his hazel eyes as he looked at her, the feel of his warm strong hand upon her own as they sat together by the fire in the parlor with all the passengers, and the intensity of their passion. Kate savored these moments and treasured them.

SIX

LIKE JUST ABOUT EVERYONE else in the months before Christmas Jack was also busy with a secret project. No one, not even Tommy, knew what it was that kept Jack occupied on short trips into town. He stealthily slipped through the woods on the frozen footpath, carrying small burlap-wrapped parcels under his arm. No one knew, that is, except the blacksmith down in Alma. But he did not breath a word.

Strangely enough, it was just about this time that one of Josie's shoes disappeared. Fortunately she had two pairs. Although she searched the hotel and questioned both Kate and Tommy, the missing shoe remained a mystery. Then, after a week, the shoe reappeared next to its mate in her upstairs bedroom closet. Though puzzled and very glad to have it back, she soon forgot about it in the preparations for the Thanksgiving meal.

The only person saddened by the prospect of the upcoming holidays was Tommy who had grown quite attached to the fairly large young turkey that strutted about the barnyard. Each June, Kate purchased a young tom for Thanksgiving dinner and fattened him up nicely with pans of table scraps left from the meals.

Somehow a friendship had sprung up between this young turkey and Tommy, and often the two spent a quiet time together resting in the small square of sunshine that fell through the uppermost barn window into the hayloft. Tommy called him Pilgrim. It was a cozy spot up there, surprisingly warm even when it was blustery out. They often caught a short nap as they listened to the rhythmic sound of Jack's horses munching their hay.

Of all the turkeys Kate had ever raised, this one seemed to behave more like a dog. When free to wander, Pilgrim followed Tommy around the yard and even into the hotel pantry, only to be shooed out by a displeased Kate. As Thanksgiving approached, Tommy began to count the days until he'd lose his friend for good. He spent many hours in the hayloft secretly feeding Pilgrim handfuls of grain from the horses' feed bin.

The next afternoon Kate went looking for Tommy and found him where she thought he might be, napping in the hayloft with the turkey. "Tommy," she called, "I want to ask you something. Come on down for a minute, would you please?" His tousled head, with bits of straw still stuck to his hair, appeared in the hole cut in the loft floor. Pilgrim also peered down at Kate, his ugly bald head cocked to the side.

"What is it, Kate?" answered Tommy, groggily.

Kate said, "I need some extra help in getting the wood pile stocked for winter." She peered at Tommy. "I know how fond you are of that turkey, Tommy. One would think it was a puppy the way it follows you about! If you would agree to top off my wood pile with split wood I will buy another turkey for the Thanksgiving dinner."

Overjoyed, Tommy picked up Pilgrim and danced about the hayloft. Pilgrim squawked wildly, and flapped his wings in Tommy's face.

Then Tommy collected himself and mildly replied, "Why, sure I'd do that Miss Kate. Me and Pilgrim are mighty happy about your kindness! I'll get started right away, I will." And the boy jumped down from the hayloft with the turkey clasped under his arm. A fair amount of loose, dusty straw followed him and they hit the floor with a crash.

Kate looked at the eager boy fondly and said, "You understand Tommy, that you can't keep every turkey every year! Just this one time I'll do it. Rough as it is here, we'd be the laughingstock of Buckskin Joe for raising pet turkeys."

The boy answered quickly, "No ma'am, this will be the only one. I promise, Kate!"

Then the two shook hands there in the log barn to seal the bargain before Tommy went out to find Jack down at the corral. As he left with his turkey strutting close behind his heels, Kate couldn't help wondering how able Tommy was to keep his promise.

NOW THAT THE WINTER SNOW was falling and blanketing the high mountains, the grazing animals were forced down to lower elevations to find food. Toward evening a small herd of mule deer grazed in the fading light of day in the meadow beside Buckskin Creek. They pawed through the thin layer of snow to reach the buried grass. This sight would become more and more familiar as winter set in. Gone was the occasional brazen bear sniffing about the garbage pits behind the houses of town, for the bears were visitors only in the warmer months of the year.

Occasionally a fox could be seen in a sunny winter meadow, his handsome red fur glowing like fire against the pristine snow and dried yellow grass as he stalked some unlucky field mouse or mole. High in the branches of a pine tree looking like a cluster of dead branches sat a porcupine, dozing for hours in the winter sun.

One evening after sunset, the stars shone brightly in the clear sky. There was no wind for a change, and though the night was cold it was somewhat pleasant compared to the usual bone chilling temperatures. On a night such as this, one could enjoy a stroll along the plank sidewalks of town without worrying about seeking refuge from the weather in the nearest doorway. But most people were settled for the evening behind closed doors, and Main Street lay deserted as stars blanketed the sky.

There was something peaceful about the scene, with soft yellow light splashing out onto the dark ground from behind lace-curtained window. The houses were clustered closely together in this town, as if for company

The next morning inside the hotel kitchen Kate and Josie peeled apples for the pies, which would be frozen in the shed until Thanksgiving Day, then baked that morning.

"I just wish we had one jar of cranberry preserves," sighed Josie. "It just doesn't seem like Thanksgiving dinner without cranberries."

Kate pushed a strand of wayward hair from her face with the back of her flour-covered hand. "Well, perhaps we can go over to the store in Breckenridge for some when Samuel comes through," she said. "Mrs. Caldwell has such things on hand during the holidays. I'd enjoy a trip over there."

She looked at Josie with excitement "Maybe we could plan a trip before Christmas to go over together! We could spend the night at the Brown Hotel, where they have a bathtub! That's where I always stay when I go over. It would be such fun if you were there too!"

In her excitement Kate stopped rolling her rounds of piecrust and pressed her white hands against the tabletop.

Josie held a half-peeled apple over the bowl and sat with her paring knife in mid-air. She looked at Kate with equal excitement, thinking of what fun a trip would be.

"That would be wonderful, Kate! I have a number of things I'd like to buy before Christmas time. And what fun we could have shopping together!"

Kate and Josie continued making their pies and discussing the possibilities of a trip to Breckenridge—what they could do there and the gifts they could purchase. The room felt comfortable with the smell of spices in the air and the snapping fire in the wood stove. Josie furrowed her brow in thought as she grated fragrant cinnamon over the heaping bowl of apple slices.

"I still can't think of what to get Jack for Christmas. What do you suppose he would like?"

"Hmmm," said Kate. "That's a hard one! Men are so difficult to buy for compared to women. And Jack's not one for gathering possessions really; what he likes best are his animals. He's always out with his dogs or fussing about the old mare."

Several minutes passed in contemplation, then Kate snapped her fingers.

"That's it Josie! Another horse! That's what Jack needs, another horse to take Buddy's place!"

Josie could see the logic in what Kate was saying. "What a perfect idea!"

Josie set her large wooden spoon on the table and looked at Kate. "But where do you suppose we could find a colt? I know nothing about buying horses."

Kate answered her with growing excitement, "My Samuel could help us! He goes through all the mining towns and stops at every livery stable. I'm sure he'd be able to find a horse we could buy for Jack. We'll ask him when he comes next Tuesday; there's over a month before Christmas so that will give us time. Perhaps we could even find a little red colt, just like Buddy! Wouldn't that be grand?"

They laid out a row of pie pans on the table and expertly covered them with discs of thin crust, which Kate trimmed and crimped with lightning speed.

"All right, Josie, I'm ready for your apples now. Why don't you fill them, and I'll start on the top crusts. Go ahead and pile them high. They'll shrink down a good bit in the baking."

Josie spooned the apple filling into the pies, and Kate was close behind her putting on the top crusts that she pinched down tightly with the flat of a fork.

"I never made pies before. I'm afraid my mother wasn't really much of a cook," said Josie, as she filled the first pie. "She spent so much of her time making dresses and working in the shop that we ate pretty simple. She was too busy to cook much, so I never did learn, except how to bake bread and roast meats. Oh, and baked beans. I'll make some for you if you want."

Josie remembered back to the days she spent as a girl in her mother's small kitchen. "My, what a long time ago that was! Kate, is this enough filling for the pie? I'm afraid I'll make a mess if I pile on much more."

Kate tucked a few apple slices here and there where small gaps were showing.

"There, that should be fine!" Kate lifted the last disc of pie dough and placed it on top of the mountain of spiced and sugared apples. With a paring knife she carved designs into each crust, twirling the pan as she did so. "You've got to let the crust breathe so it doesn't break the seam and leak juice as it's baking," Kate explained to Josie, who watched raptly.

"All right, we're finished! The pies are ready for Thanksgiving, and all I have to do is bake them on that morning before the dinner. It saves such a lot of trouble making them ahead of time. There are some benefits to the cold up here," she said as she put two pies on Josie's hands and took two her self. "It's not everywhere that you can freeze ten pies and an elk haunch in a storage shed five months of the year!" When all the pies were safely stacked on shelves in the shed, they covered the pies with clean white flour sacks before they left and bolted the shed door closed. Kate dusted the flour off her hands with her apron before smoothing several curls back from her face. She sat down in one of the kitchen chairs and breathed a deep, satisfied sigh.

"Have a seat, Josie, I want to think more about this horse for Jack." She chewed her lip thoughtfully and said, "You know, it being such a large gift and all, I think it might be appropriate for a few of us to buy it together for him. Would you mind that Josie, if it wasn't just from you yourself?" She smiled rather mischievously and added, "Being that he's your sweetheart and all?" Kate giggled at the slow blush that crept over Josie's cheeks. Josie stared fixedly at the sugar bowl on the table in front of her.

"No, that would be fine! Jack would like it so much more if he knew it was from all of us, not just me. Why, compared to everyone else here he barely knows me!" She looked out the small paned window above the kitchen sink towards Jack's cabin. Her voice was soft as she said, "He's such a nice man, and does so much for everyone without even asking for anything. He just drifts away afterward as if he doesn't want to be noticed." She looked at Kate and smiled. "Believe it or not, it's possible that he is even shyer than I am!"

As they cleared up from making their pies the mid-afternoon sun streamed across the room through the small kitchen window. Under the table several kittens rolled happily on the floor, batting at the stray apple peels that had fallen from the table.

Josie wiped the table with a clean flour sackcloth as Kate washed out the mixing bowls in the sink.

Josie handed Kate the cloth and then quickly hugged her friend. "Kate, you are the best friend that I've ever had. I'm so glad now that I came here and found such good people. This place feels like my home, more than St. Louis ever did."

Kate squeezed her back and smiled at Josie, "I'm glad you've come too, Josie. You were just what we all needed here. You know, ever since I came here I've felt the same way as you. Folks here draw together close just like they are family. Maybe it's living in the mountains that make it so. We need each other more than folks do in the cities, just to survive."

She lifted the dishes from the wash pan and set them to dry on the high wooden counter that ran along the wall to the pantry. Kate spoke thoughtfully. "I don't think I could leave this town and go back to city life again. Buckskin Joe suits me just fine."

Kate untied her apron and hung it on a nail beside the dishes. She looked out the window into the bright sunshine. "My, what a fine day it is still! Josie, let's take a walk before it gets too late, shall we? There's plenty of time before we have to think about starting dinner. If you would come with me, we could walk up to Windy Ridge! There's a grand view of the South Park there."

Josie answered, "That sounds wonderful Kate!" Secretly she hoped they'd run into Jack.

Josie and Kate changed their clothes and were ready to go on their outing in no time. On Main Street they headed up the road under the canopy of tall pines toward the snowy peaks of the Mosquito Range, leaving their worries, if they had any, behind for the duration of their outing.

After twenty minutes of brisk walking they reached the top of the ridge where the trees opened up and revealed a breathtaking view of the Great South Park. The women sat down on a large smooth rock to bask in the warm sunshine.

"Isn't this lovely?" exclaimed Kate as she looked out across the miles and miles of flat prairie with the hazy mountains rising like ocean waves in the distance. "It's so good to get up here again, I'd not trade living here for the world." Kate sat quietly after she spoke, and breathed deeply of the cool, pine scented air.

"What if you were in love with someone who didn't want to stay here? Would you leave then?" asked Josie.

"I wouldn't if it meant going back to London! I'll never go back there as long as I live—to stay, that is. I couldn't stand to live in a big city again," said Kate.

"What if Samuel asked you to marry him, would you leave then?" Josie asked with a teasing grin.

"What if Jack asked you, Josie? Would you follow him where ever he wanted to go?" asked Kate.

"I don't know. I like Jack well enough, but something inside me doesn't want to follow after a man. What if things went bad and you had given up everything to go with him? It's nothing against Jack, I would think the same about going away with any man," said Josie seriously.

"I know what you mean, it seems like bad luck to give up your independence to be with someone. If I left the hotel I would have nothing, and I would need a man to take care of me. I'm not sure I want to need someone that badly. It could ruin things," said Kate.

"Yes, I've thought of that too! On the one hand you love someone, but you don't want to need him so much that you can't get along on your own. There's no way out unless you want to be an old maid!" said Josie.

They laughed hilariously, for neither one of them dreamed of ending up as an old maid.

All too soon the sun began it's descent behind the mountains to the west, and the shadows across the meadow near town grew long. Cows grazed contentedly as the women hurried past them toward home when they remembered dinner still needed preparing.

Josie helped Kate make the dinner for the hotel guests. Later, Kate covered the pot of elk stew and set it on the back of the stove to simmer, then left the kitchen and put on her coat and hat. As she walked down the hill to the bakery she saw in the sky one pink cloud, thin as a ribbon, stretched above the horizon where it caught the rays of the setting sun.

"Evening, Tim!" Kate called, as she came through the bakery door. A string of small brass bells tied to the door jingled cheerfully. "I see you're all ready for the holidays here," Kate said, indicating the bells. "I'm afraid you've got me beat, unless my Thanksgiving pies count. They're made and freezing at this very moment."

Tim's deep brown eyes were mischievous. "Why then, it's a dead tie, Kate. I'm making all my pies tomorrow. Mostly squash."

Kate stepped behind the counter and went into the back room of the bakery where Tim was mixing up a batch of bread dough. Most visitors ended up in the kitchen to visit with the baker, whether it was Chris or Tim. They squeezed in among the shelves full of pans, bins and sacks of ingredients stacked on the floor.

"Kate, would you be kind enough to pass me the cinnamon from the shelf behind you there?" Tim asked, as he wiped his flour-covered hands on his long white apron. "Thank you kindly," he said as he took it from her and shook the tin over the contents in the large mixing bowl. The mass turned reddish brown.

"Smells wonderful, sweet rolls, huh?" asked Kate.

He rolled his eyes and grinned. Can't keep these around for long. Seems they're everyone's favorite."

He mixed with energetic strokes, and then dumped the dough onto the floured counter in front of him. "You know Kate, it sure is nice to have your beautiful face in my kitchen here. And I've heard tell that you're just about as good a baker as me!" He looked pointedly at her. "We could use another baker around here and someone prettier than Chris. Jack might never speak to me again, but it is a price I'd be willing pay to have you by my side here at the bakery!"

Kate threw her head back and laughed. She'd been hearing this for three years and knew that Tim's offer was in jest. Everyone knew how loyal she was to Jack. "Tim, you just never quit, do you? Much as I'd like to come and have the pleasure of your company, I dare say I'd be hard pressed to leave the hotel. I do appreciate your offer, though. It is most flattering."

She squeezed his elbow fondly. "Oh my! In all this visiting I clean forgot why I came down! I need two dozen dinner rolls for tonight, if I may." She laughed again and shook her head, as she said, "You know Tim, you'd lose money if I worked for you because we'd chat away the day and leave the work undone, wouldn't we!"

Tim shook his head back and forth and grinned as he counted out twenty-four rolls into a sack for Kate. "I suppose you're right there, Kate, but it sure would be fun, wouldn't it!"

Coming to see Tim always put a lift in Kate's day. She knew that given the chance he would pursue her romantically, and what woman did not find that complimentary?

"It's been a pleasure, Tim," said Kate with her hand on the doorknob. "Don't be a stranger. Come down and see us at the hotel sometime. It's not fair that I should always have to be the one to come and see you!" And with that, she left with a flourish and closed the bakery door with a satisfying bang and a jingle of bells.

SEVEN

THANKSGIVING WAS unseasonably warm. The temperatures in the afternoon rose above sixty degrees, and the people of Buckskin Joe shook their heads in bewilderment, not quite knowing what to make of the temperatures. Summer and winter seemed to have traded places this year.

The stage arrived as usual on Tuesday afternoon; and Samuel always laid over for several nights during the holidays so that all could enjoy a relaxing time of visiting and feasting in the Thanksgiving tradition. None was happier than Kate, who clung to Samuel's arm tightly between her kitchen duties, thrilled she was to have him near for two whole days. Tommy and Pilgrim were perhaps the most grateful of all. Together they enjoyed a plate of sage stuffing out in the barn on Thanksgiving afternoon.

After dinner some passengers rocked slowly in creaking chairs near the crackling wood stove. They exchanged stories of childhood Thanksgivings, the new president, and the price of gold. Eventually they turned to the unusual weather. One old man warned "Mark my words, don't let this nice spell fool you. The weather's gonna take a turn and when it does it'll be nasty!"

During the next few days, instead of snowshoes and sleds, the townspeople unpacked their warm weather clothes and strolled leisurely under the pleasant sunshine of the afternoons. The children took turns trotting in circles round Jack's corral on big Ty, using a piece of twine for reins. As they went round and round on the old horse, the dust rose in great clouds. In a normal year by November the corral would be buried as high as the horses' knees under hard, crusty snow.

A somewhat disoriented Kate felt the urge to fuss with her flowerpots. She took her geranium off the kitchen shelf and pulled off the brown dead leaves. She thought about re-potting it. Josie, feeling restless, became bored with her book and sat idly watching Kate pluck the dead leaves from the spindly plant.

"It's certainly fine weather for a picnic. Perhaps we should pack up some food and head up to the lake before the snow decides to come back. We may never have a chance again to have a picnic so close to December," said Josie.

Kate looked up from her geranium plant with interest. "That sounds like a fine idea, Josie! There's certainly enough turkey left to make some nice sandwiches. Why don't we ask Jack if he would like to come along. We have so much food left from Thanksgiving dinner that I don't really have to cook for two more days, except for breakfasts. I'll wrap some pie and we could even bring some bottles of beer!"

Excited by the prospect of an outing, the two women hurried about the kitchen and packed a fine picnic basket. Tommy invited Jack, and the four of them set off on foot up Buckskin Road accompanied by Jack's dogs that seemed overjoyed by this unexpected adventure up the mountain.

Once they arrived at the lake, they stretched lazily on a large, woolen blanket beside the rippling blue water. They feasted hungrily on the thick turkey sandwiches and slices of cold apple pie, washing it all down with cold bottles of Jack's homemade beer.

"Ah, this is the life," sighed Kate, contentedly. "Just think, usually we'd be freezing to the death, trying to warm ourselves around the wood stove during a blizzard." She lifted her face to catch the warm sun, feeling that delicious heat upon her skin.

"Feels as though we might be in California, from all I've heard of it," said Jack. "This weather suits me just fine."

He took a substantial swallow from his bottle of beer. Tommy tossed chunks of wood into the still waters of the lake for the dog to retrieve. Not seeming to mind the frigid waters of the high mountain lake, Nipper paddled furiously after the floating prize, then brought it back in his mouth and dropped it in the tall sedge grass at Tommy's feet.

An occasional fish broke the lake's surface. I should have brought some fishing line," said Jack. "We could have had trout for dinner." He chewed absently on a stem of yellow meadow grass as he looked out across the lake. "I should be fishing." Jack turned his head aside as he spit out the wood-like remnants of the grass stem and then picked a new thick stalk, which he began to chew. "I much prefer to do my fishing on a nice warm day like today," he continued. "There's enough suffering the cold up here without going out of my way to freeze while ice fishing. I don't fancy trout badly enough that I need to eat it twelve months of a year!" He leaned comfortably back on his elbows as he took another sip from his brown bottle.

Josie, who was not at all used to drinking any type of alcohol, sipped cautiously of the foaming, amber liquid in her glass jar.

"Hmm, it's interesting," she commented, trying to be polite. She wrinkled her nose and wondered how Kate and Jack could enjoy drinking such quantities of the distasteful stuff. Perhaps one gets used to it over time, she supposed. Venturing another sip, it seemed to taste a little better this time. The carbonation chased the taste away and left her tongue tingling strangely.

Kate reclined, her face completely shaded beneath her wide-brimmed straw hat. "Perhaps I should move down south to California. I'm sure I could get used to this weather all year with no trouble at all." She yawned and closed her eyes.

Jack shook his head in disagreement. "Not me! I've been through a good part of the gold country of California, and it's as strange a place as you'll ever find. No seasons—it just stays about the same all year. That's fine for some, but I'd miss the snow."

He pushed his brown felt hat back upon his forehead and scratched his forehead. "Once it gets too easy for a man to make a living you get all them lazy sorts down there and before you know it the town's full of nothing but worthless old drunks. Up here the cold will kill a man who's too lazy to provide for himself."

He turned toward Kate and said jokingly, "I don't think you'd like it there, Kate. Surely you'd miss your wildflowers!"

Kate sighed and opened her eyes. She rolled onto her elbows. "Oh, I suppose you're right. But it doesn't hurt to dream, does it? Besides, you're right. I'd just grow fat and lazy in such a place. Here the wind blows so cold you can't keep fat on your bones even if you try!" She laughed, not really being the type of woman who worried about her figure.

While she was not as thin and fine-boned as Josie, her natural waist had not been squeezed inside a corset for years. "Well like they say, you always want what you don't have, but I suppose even California has its problems too, ones we just don't know about."

Seeing Josie look at Jack, Kate decided a nice walk would be in order. Give them lovebirds a bit of privacy, she thought. She rose stiffly from the blanket and brushed the bits of dried weeds and grass from her skirt. "Come on, Tommy. I do believe we'll take a little walk before we head back to town. You two enjoy yourselves. Tommy and I will see if we can hunt down some marmots in the rock field above the lake."

Kate and Tommy set off on the worn footpath through the thick sedge grass to the small stream that tumbled through the rock field. The water sprang from an underground source and gathered force on its way downhill through a field of sharp slag rock. The rock was stained an unnatural bright orange from the chemical the miners used to extract gold ore.

Amongst the rocky piles, an occasional brown furry head poked up, only to disappear. The marmots warned their communities of danger, emitting a series of high-pitched chirping noises which nearly drove the two dogs mad. Try as they might, they weren't quick enough to catch the elusive creatures, and roamed around with their noses rooting in the small spaces between the rocks, sniffing the scent of the marmots.

After Kate and Tommy disappeared behind the bog birch bushes, a feeling of peace settled over Josie and Jack who sat on the blanket by the water's edge in the fading light.

Without speaking a word, Jack looked into Josie's eyes and took her small, smooth hand in his large work-roughened hand. She returned his gaze steadily, showing no signs of unease at this overture.

Jack knew he didn't have very long before Kate and Tommy would return. Jack bent his face tentatively toward hers. She met his kiss with an intensity that surprised her. Then she nestled her head against his shoulder and closed her eyes. It felt good to feel a man's strength again. Horace peeked from behind a gray memory, but Jack sent him on his way. She finally felt free of him. She had Jack beside her now. After a while she stirred from her peaceful position when she heard Kate and Tommy rustling through the bushes.

Kate carried a large bunch of branches that were thick with large, red berries. "Look what we found to decorate the hotel!" she exclaimed.

Tommy also had an armload of branches, and once they came closer, Josie saw what she thought were berries looked more liked small, crimson apples.

"Why, whatever are those, Kate?" she asked.

Kate laughed, surprised that Josie didn't recognize these most common plants. "They're wild rose hips, Josie! Won't they look splendid on the stair banister with the pine boughs, and around the entry to the parlor? Look how many Tommy has! I've never thought of using these before, and there's such a lot of them where the stream feeds into the lake." Kate's cheeks glowed as red as the rose hips she had gathered.

Josie thought it was the prettiest she'd ever seen her. "Those are lovely! What a clever idea to use them for decorations!" Then she stood and reached for Jack, who had risen beside her.

Jack, who had picked up the blanket, said, "The sun is about gone. I suppose we'd best be getting back?"

The others nodded in agreement and the small group prepared to head back to town before night fell. They rolled up the blanket and packed the basket full of the rose branches.

Kate sighed contentedly, as they headed down below the lake along the deeply rutted road to Buckskin Joe. "What a wonderful afternoon!

It's not every day we have such a summer's day picnic!" The others agreed, it had been a very fine afternoon indeed.

The next day however, changes came about in the weather. Although the air was still unseasonably warm, ferocious winds began to rise in the late morning. By the late afternoon a person could not walk outside without shielding his eyes from the blowing sand and grit. Even Jack's old dog Nipper could not make his way over to the barn from the corral without squeezing his eyes tightly shut while his long black ears rose rather comically in the stiff wind. Nine inches of snow fell that night.

The flow of miners through town lessened considerably during the winter months, almost down to nothing. The late arrival of winter this year had caused quite a number of the miners to have another go at their claims. The cold snap drove them down to town just as it drove the pronghorn, elk and deer to lower feeding grounds. Only a handful of toughened individuals stuck out the entire winter working their claims. They lived in tiny log cabins chinked with mud and buried to the roof in snow.

Not all these men survived through the winter however. When the thaws of spring came and the first horses made their slow way up through the high, muddy trails where the claims lay, an unlucky miner or two often was found dead in or near his cabin or sometimes not at all. Whether from starvation, cold, or wild animal attack, their deaths told the harsh story of a miner's life.

In spite of the hardships and dangers, these independent men willingly chose this reclusive life over an existence within the confines of a city or town. They were free from the annoying meddling of other people and enjoyed the challenge of surviving by their wits. And they were happy with their life.

Then when this early December blizzard hit, it brought all but a handful of the toughest miners down to the comforts and shelter of town. Life in town was anything but quiet. Deprived of women, whiskey and fellowship for so long, the gold burned holes in their pockets and quickly found a new home in the tills of the sporting houses and saloons. Many a round of whiskey was bought.

❦

ONE EVENING, A WEEK after the snow fell, Tommy was helping Jack roll out the empty wooden beer kegs from the saloon. A nearly toothless and drunk miner sitting at the bar took a sudden interest in the boy. As

Tommy passed near him, the miner put his hand on the boy's shoulder.

"Bit young to be around the likes of this place, ain't ya boy?" he bellowed into Tommy's ear. "Ah remember when ah was yer age, young feller. S'when ah had my first whore. You had one yit, boy?"

Tommy pulled back from the miner's leering face, the man's breath reeking of whiskey. It reminded him unpleasantly of his father. The miner stood up with some difficulty then stumbled slightly.

Tommy was too embarrassed to answer the man, and he looked anxiously across the noisy room toward Jack.

But Jack was busy, absorbed in conversation with some friends he had not seen in months—miners on a claim up Mosquito Gulch. Tommy would have like to slip past the rude miner, but the man's hand was still clamped to his shoulder.

"Shots fer all!" hollered the miner as he plunked down a sizable pile of coins on the worn wooden bar. A boisterous group of men quickly clustered around the miner. The barkeep lined small whiskey glasses in front of the group, and the miner gave Tommy a slap across the shoulder that about knocked him to his knees.

"Drink up, boy! It'll put hair on yer chest!" he hollered, as he looked expectantly at Tommy.

Everyone laughed heartily and looked knowingly at one another. With a look of resignation the boy reached for the glass and raised it to his lips with a trembling hand. He took a small sip and immediately began to cough violently.

"Ya got t'drink it in one swaller, boy!" the old man yelled impatiently, slamming his fist on the bar in exasperation, causing a few of the coins to clink upon the floor. "Whiskey ain't fer sippin!"

Feeling that he might as well go ahead and drink the stuff and get out of there, Tommy put the glass to his lips again and poured the offensive liquid down his throat in one gulp. This time his coughing spasm was so bad that Tommy thought he was about to vomit the drink all over the saloon floor.

The noise finally attracted the attention of Jack, who saw Tommy clinging to the bar with whiskey darkening the front of his shirt. Jack stalked across the crowded room and jerked the drunken old miner to his feet by the collar of his dirty coat. Jack was not a man to anger easily, but when he did, it was a sight to behold. Ever since Tommy had been left abandoned in Buckskin Joe, Jack had taken the boy under his wing.

"I should smash you into the floor for what you did to that boy, you old drunk!" Jack hissed through clenched teeth. His rough cheek twitched as he glared into the frightened man's eyes. He jerked the man's collar a few inches closer and said, "You better make yourself plenty scarce." With a sudden movement Jack shoved the old man against the bar. "Git!" The old man didn't need to be told twice.

The saloon was silent as Jack confronted the old miner, and a space was cleared as Jack and Tommy left. It was a rare event to see Jack angry. And Tommy wouldn't forget the experience either.

That same week, Samuel drove his team through the last stormy stretch of the stage route before finally reaching Buckskin Joe. The strong and persistent wind blew the snow in a peculiar manner causing it to flow eerily across the prairie, hovering inches from the ground. It was like a great white sheet stretched across the wide expanse of the South Park, pinned down at the corners and rippling in the wind.

It had been a long hard trip from Tin Cup Pass up the valley to Buena Vista where Samuel had spent the night. The last several snowfalls had left certain sections of the road nearly impossible to pass through, tripling the usual length of the trip. Ten hours earlier he had hitched the fresh team up for the last leg of the route over Trout Creek Pass. As the tired horses struggled through windswept snow banks Samuel occupied his mind with the happy thought that he would see Kate tonight. It kept his spirits up.

The stage finally arrived in Buckskin Joe, and the warm yellow light that fell in long rectangles across the dark snowy road beckoned invitingly. Although Samuel was chilled to the bone and quite tired, his heart stirred with excitement. Before he had hitched his team to the post, the hotel door burst open and Kate appeared on the porch wrapped in a dark woolen shawl.

"Samuel! You're finally here! I've been watching for hours. She stepped lightly down the steps and hugged him, nuzzling her face into his neck. "I've kept dinner warm for you on the stove."

Samuel gave Kate an affectionate squeeze and kissed her softly, glad to be with her again. As he stepped into the road to see to the horses, he looked back at her, the dim light casting a halo around her brown curly hair.

Although Kate was not strikingly beautiful, she possessed a certain vitality that made her stand out from all the rest. It was apparent in the warmth of her laughter and the easy, comforting touch of her hand upon another's. There was a lack of self-consciousness about her that made her actions genuine and true. Kate was a most trusted and admired woman in Buckskin Joe. He knew he was a fool for not asking her to marry him, what if another man beat him to it?

These thoughts went through Samuel's mind as he stood beside his horses, holding the reins in his hand. The sweat on their large bodies had cooled, and their thick, winter hair was curled and stiffening.

"I'll be in shortly, Kate. They're cooled down enough for their oats now. Perhaps you'd like to get a coat and come out to the barn with me?" He did not take his eyes from her face as he spoke, so happy he was to see her again.

"Let me get my coat!" said Kate. The heavy door banged closed behind her as she dashed inside.

Kate joined him moments later inside the shelter of the log barn lit softly by the glow of Samuel's kerosene lantern that hung by a nail above the grain bin. The horses were already eating their oats, and the methodical sound of their chewing filled the barn. Samuel was loading the hayracks to the top with sweet-smelling green hay. He turned when he heard Kate come in. Kate leaned against the wooden rails which separated the horses from the storage area.

"I brought a few old woolen blankets over in case you wanted them for the horses. They're worn but still usable. We just purchased all new blankets for the hotel. Could you use them, Samuel?"

Samuel set the pitchfork against the wall and came over to where Kate was standing.

"Kate, you'll spoil us all! The horses won't want to leave Buckskin Joe any more than I will tomorrow morning." He gave her a knowing glance then said, "Climb over here with me, and let's see how they like their new coats."

He took the blankets from her and set them down, then grasped her hands as she gingerly climbed over the makeshift fence. She jumped from the top rail down to the dirt floor below, her skirt filling with air as she landed. Kate laughed merrily and fell against Samuel. He kissed her upon the cheek affectionately and then unfolded one of the blankets.

"Kate, you take hold of that side and help me get this blanket on Mister."

Together they blanketed the first horse and then the second. So intent were the horses upon their feed they gave no notice of their new attire.

Samuel turned to Kate and said, "Well, now that the horses are set for a good night, shall we go and have one ourselves?"

Kate could hardly contain her excitement as the two of them left the darkened barn behind. Samuel held the kerosene lantern high to illuminate the dark, snowy path that led to the hotel.

Earlier, Kate had set a place for Samuel at the end of the long dining table next to the wood stove. Now, the swinging doors that separated the dining room from the kitchen were closed so that no curious guest might wander in. Kate had left a large pot of mulled wine on the back of the stove in the parlor and a tray of cups for the guests to serve themselves. A pan of fresh gingerbread was set out also for a late night snack.

Kate lit the small lamp on the sideboard and served Samuel a full bowl of elk stew. Then she pulled a plate of steaming cornbread and a dish of bubbling brown beans from the oven.

"Would you like a cup of tea with your dinner, Samuel, or a glass of beer?"

Samuel had just washed his hands in a bucket of fresh water, and dried them on a clean towel. After draping the towel over the side of the bucket, he went over to where Kate was standing by the stove.

"You're too good to be true, Kate. I'll never know what luck brought you into my life." He took her hands in his. "I never imagined the day when I would hear myself saying to anyone that I needed them, but I dare say I'm feeling that way about you, and more each time I see you." He bent his prickly whiskered face to kiss her.

Kate answered him with a catch in her throat, "I've been feeling the same way too, Samuel."

She leaned against his wide chest and closed her eyes for a moment, glad to feel him close again. He put his arms around her and held her tightly, and they hugged each other.

The dim light from the small oil lamp flickered, causing shadows to move against the dark wood wall. The dinner that Kate had kept warm was now getting cold.

"Let's go upstairs, Kate. I'll eat later." Samuel whispered into her ear.

Then the two slipped quietly out of the kitchen and up the stairs to Kate's room, leaving Samuel's untouched dinner on the table.

To Samuel's disappointment, it didn't snow enough that night to delay the stage for one more day. He lay under fresh flannel sheets and several woolen blankets. A beautiful hand-stitched quilt was laid on top. A jar of freshly cut juniper and spruce branches tied with a red silk ribbon was on the lowboy dresser under the window. He had smelled the fresh, sharp scent of the pinesap in the cold air when he awoke at first light.

The room was part of Kate's private quarters, most often used as a sitting room for sewing or reading. She kept a bed there for use when the hotel rooms were full, or if a single lady happened to be traveling on the stage.

Although Kate secretly visited Samuel in this room, her sense of propriety would never allow her to stay with him all night. Usually, Samuel would drift off to sleep with Kate's head nestled under his chin and her warm body curled against his. In the morning she was always gone.

Samuel sniffed. The wonderful aroma of brewing coffee and frying bacon that drifted up the stairs from the kitchen. He knew Kate would be busy getting ready for the day's business.

With the sheets up to his nose, his eyes traveled slowly about the high-ceilinged room, taking in the details. There was a large white porcelain washbowl and pitcher on the dresser. A framed fox hunting print of men in red coats riding long legged horses over fences behind a pack hounds hung on the light blue and white floral-papered wall. Samuel was more accustomed to rough planked walls, perhaps lined with newspaper to keep out the wind. This room was very feminine, and it made him feel a bit strange.

Through the open doorway, which led to the connected sitting room, Samuel could see the prickly, green horsehair love seat against the far wall. Several small, colorful braided rugs lay on the unpainted wooden floor, and long white lace curtains hung well below the sill of the single tall window which looked westward toward the Continental Divide.

From his bed, Samuel could see a splendid view of the Mosquito Mountains shining pure white under a clear and bright blue sky. Even though the fair weather meant that he would have no excuse to stay in Buckskin Joe another night, Samuel could not help feeling his spirits lift at seeing such a beautiful sight. It would be a fine day to drive the stage loaded with passengers up over Hoosier Pass and down into the Blue River Valley.

While he was lost in thought in the cheerful, sun-filled room, he heard three soft knocks on the door.

He called out. "Who is it?"

The door opened a few inches, and Kate poked her head in. "Are you decent? I haven't caught you dressing, have I?" She laughed at his hair sticking out every which way.

She came over to the bed and kissed him. "You best wake up, sleepy head. Your breakfast is hot and waiting, and Josie and I have a proposition for you. If you had room for me and Josie, we'd like to ride to with you. We've been planning a trip to Breckenridge for some time. We'd like to spend the night at the Brown Hotel and also do a bit of shopping."

Samuel had the quilt pulled up to his chin, and he had a mischievous look on his face. "Why, certainly you ladies are welcome to ride over with me. I'll even let you ride for free if I might have a bath at the Brown Hotel. In fact, I would pay a nice bit of change if you were to share your bath with me!"

Kate jumped on the bed and poked playfully at his stomach. "You are naughty! What kind of lady do you take me for? I'm not sure you deserve this fine breakfast I've cooked up downstairs!" She rose from the bed and said, "Anyhow, there won't be any food left at all if you don't get your handsome self dressed and down there before Jack and Tommy eat it all. Not to mention the guests!"

Kate stopped at the door looking over her shoulder at him before she left the room. Speaking in a softer, more intimate tone she said, "Sure is nice having you here, Samuel." She paused, fixing a picture of him in bed under her roof, so she could keep him there in her memory at least. Then she left the room.

A few hours later, after Samuel had rearranged some sacks and boxes from inside to the top of the stagecoach, the two excited women climbed aboard with their overnight bags. Josie and Kate sat on either side of Samuel. Usually no one sat with him on the driver's seat except for Butch, his small, black mutt. The happy group set off toward Hoosier Pass in the highest of spirits. Due to the crowded conditions, Butch rode on Kate's lap, his long black ears flapping in the breeze as they jostled down the road out of Buckskin Joe.

In this remote mountain life where travel was difficult due to bad weather and rough terrain, most people did not often venture far from Buckskin Joe. Josie was anxious to see Breckenridge, which she had heard so much about from Kate. She had not been out of Buckskin Joe since her arrival the previous March.

The team of strong bays pulled the coach slowly but steadily up the final ascent to the highest point of their journey over the Continental Divide, where the white-covered peaks of Mount Lincoln and Mount Bross rose to magnificent heights above the Blue River Valley to the north and the Great South Park to the south. On their way up the pass they saw many trains of burros tied nose to tail led by the miners who were traveling to their claims on the mountainsides.

These small animals with their ridiculously large ears could haul an amazingly heavy load. Some of the burros carried bundles and sacks of supplies that were stacked high on their backs. One train of burros hauled many long, wooden beams to be used for supporting the deep mine tunnels, which were dug into the mountain. The heavy beams were a good ten feet longer than the animals.

Without these sturdy little creatures it would have been impossible for the miners to haul supplies and equipment up the mountainside, for the burros maneuvered on trails where wagon teams were inaccessible.

Some of the miners who worked their small claims alone had been known to share their huts with their four-legged companions during the harshest months of the winter. A man could get mighty lonely in the dark days of winter, and a burro was a better companion than none at all. And the burro added warmth to a tiny space. To some men living with a burro was preferable to another person. Miners could be a peculiar lot.

⌀

BY THE TIME the stage arrived in Breckenridge, the lights of town were glowing softly in the dusk. The Ten Mile Mountain Range stretched along the western horizon, and Josie was awestruck by the beauty of the uninterrupted row of white mountain peaks. Breckenridge was perched upon a cleared sloping hillside above the river valley where the view of the mountains was open and unobscured by trees or hills.

Josie was quite taken with her first sight of the bustling mining town with its crowded streets and numerous shops, restaurants and hotels. She exclaimed to Kate, "I can't wait to walk through town and see the shops! It's been so long since I've been in a real dressmaker's shop."

Josie looked especially pretty when she was excited, with spots of color on her flushed cheeks and a sparkle in her dark blue eyes. She squeezed her friend's hand as she they passed in front of the tall and box-shaped false storefronts on Main Street.

"Where is the Brown Hotel?" she asked Kate. "Are we near it yet?"

Kate answered with equal excitement, "It's just a few blocks up this hill, off Main Street. Oh Josie, We're going to have so much fun! I am glad that we came!"

Samuel couldn't have been prouder as he pulled his coach to a stop in front of the two story Victorian hotel where the ornate porch railings were decorated with pine boughs and red ribbons for the holidays. He helped the two women down from their high seats and escorted them, one on each arm, into the hotel.

As soon as they walked through the entrance, the beaming hotel proprietor greeted them. "Why Samuel, you old devil, isn't one beauty enough for you?" the short, stout man joked. "I say, you may be forced to share one of them with me!" George linked his arm with Kate's. "My dear, it is a pleasure, as always, to see you again! It's been far too long since you visited our hotel!" The jovial man kissed her hand with great ceremony. "Perhaps this time I'll convince you to move to civilization and run my kitchen. Your talents are wasted on those rough miners!"

Kate's shook her head and laughed. "Now, George, you know Jack couldn't run the hotel without me!"

George shook his round shiny head and sighed in feigned defeat. He turned his benevolent face toward Josie. "Well then, perhaps I'll have better luck with your charming friend. Aren't you going to introduce us?" He held out his hand.

Josie took his pudgy hand. "It's Miss Pye, sir. Mr. Brown, I presume?"

He bowed over her hand before solemnly correcting her. "You must call me George, Miss Pye, or I shall be most deeply offended. All my friends do. And I do insist that we be friends." After giving her hand a squeeze, he turned to Samuel, who had been watching the proceedings with an amused expression.

"Samuel!" he bellowed. "I shall take charge of these beautiful ladies while you fetch their bags. Please, join us in the bar for some champagne; we must toast the season, and your arrival here in Breckenridge, ladies!"

He ushered the two women from the ornate lobby into the warm and low-ceilinged bar room, which was decorated with fine polished dark wood and many ornate glass lamps. He seated them at the long bar in front of a polished mirror. The wood of the counter glowed deep reddish brown in the soft light of the room, and Josie was slightly overwhelmed by the richness of the surroundings. It had been quite a while since she had sat in such a luxuriously appointed room. Certainly nothing in Buckskin Joe compared with this!

George snapped his fingers and two mugs of steaming hot buttered rum appeared in front of Josie and Kate. "A little drink to take the chill of traveling from you, ladies! Warm your fingers on those while I go find the missus and tell her you are here."

He disappeared through a narrow doorway draped with a dark red velvet curtain. They could hear him calling, "Bessie, come along! I've a surprise for you! You'll never guess who's come for a visit!"

Before Kate or Josie had taken a sip from their drinks, he reappeared through the curtain, followed by his equally plump and cheerful wife.

"My land! If it's not Kate! Where have you been keeping yourself so long? It's so good to see your smiling face again!" She embraced Kate, and then kissed her on the cheek. "And who is your lovely companion? Do introduce me!"

Josie extended her hand shyly toward the newcomer, "I'm Miss Pye, ma'am. Pleased to make your acquaintance. You have a lovely hotel!"

Bessie Brown squeezed Josie's hand tightly in her own, and then hugged her, as if she were a long lost member of the family.

Formalities taken care of, Bessie bustled about the bar, serving the visitors oysters on real china plates, hot fresh biscuits and raspberry preserves, pickled vegetables and smoked fish. Samuel joined the merry party, shaking a light dusting of snow from his hat and coat before he took a seat at the bar, beside Kate.

"Bessie, you're spoiling us! How will we ever convince the ladies to return back to the wilds of Buckskin Joe after such treatment as this?"

He took a heaping forkful of oysters and closed his eyes as he tasted them. "I'll remember this meal when I'm out in the middle of nowhere freezing on the stage. Oysters! Where ever did you get them?"

Bessie Brown beamed at Samuel as she stood before him with a steaming dish of creamed potatoes. "George got them for me on his last trip to Denver. They come from back east. I've always loved oysters!"

As twilight grew, more guests began to fill the bar. A fire crackled in the large brick fireplace and bright flames licked the sides of the flue. Outside the snow had begun to fall steadily, quieting the world and increasing the sense of warmth and comfort inside.

"A toast!" bellowed Mr. Brown, as he stood on a barstool. He raised his glass high.

"A toast to the season and to friendship!" A cheer went up, and the room was filled with the sound of clinking glasses.

Samuel grasped Kate's hand in his. "Will you marry me?" he said into her ear over the din of the room.

She turned toward him, overcome with happiness.

"Yes!"

EIGHT

As CHRISTMAS DREW NEARER, the level of excitement in Buckskin Joe grew. Perhaps the biggest secret was Jack's gift—the sorrel colt with the crooked white stripe running down his nose, hidden at a farm in Fairplay.

The plan was to bring the colt over on Christmas Eve and put him into Jack's corral under the cover of darkness. The next morning, Jack would come out and find his new horse waiting for him. The only concern was that Jack's old bay mare might give the secret away by neighing in excitement over the arrival of her new stable mate, and cause Jack to come out before the appointed time.

So a new plan was devised. There would be the Christmas Eve dance at the schoolhouse. Samuel would wait until Jack had left his cabin for the dance, and then bring the colt into the corral from the barn in Buckskin Joe, where it would be hidden that day. All of Jack Herndon's friends winked at each other that week with knowing grins on their faces. They couldn't wait for Christmas morning.

Two days before Christmas, dawn broke cold and clear, with a fresh cover of white on the ground. Today the new colt would be brought from Fairplay and hidden in a neighbor's barn in Buckskin Joe until the next evening.

For weeks Kate and Josie had spent every spare moment in Kate's sitting room, sewing a saddle blanket for Jack's new horse. They were going to wrap it before the Christmas Eve party, where, as was the tradition, a gift exchange would take place after the dance.

The saddle blanket was sewn from a beautiful length of white wool with black and brown stripes, woven by a Ute Indian from the South Park. Samuel had traded a large jar of molasses for it when he had camped with the Indian at the salt spring by Trout Creek Pass.

❧

CHRISTMAS EVE FINALLY ARRIVED. Jack rode his old bay mare up into the forest and cut a large, bushy blue spruce for the party. He dragged the tree back down through the woods with a rope tied to his saddle horn.

Kate and Josie met him at the hotel and helped him carry it into the front parlor. After sawing a few inches off the stump, they balanced the tree in a large bucket that was held in place by several large blocks of wood. Then they attached wires to small nails in the wall and tied the wires to several branches. This steadied the tree. Kate covered the bucket and the wood blocks with an old white sheet, and filled the bucket with a pitcher of sugar water. They stood back to admire their work. Even without ornaments, the tree was beautiful.

People came to Buckskin Joe from the neighboring towns of Alma and Fairplay, and even as far away as Como and Hamilton for the annual Christmas Eve dance and dinner. It was the greatest social event of the year. Everyone took pains to look their finest. Even the roughest bachelor miners, took their annual bath, scrubbing away the permanent layer of Rocky Mountain dust off their skin. Along with a clean shirt they appeared at he party with freshly nicked and shaven chins sporting wrinkled but clean white shirts and string bow ties. The excitement in the air was contagious, and hugs and greetings were liberally exchanged.

The students' benches had been pushed back against the walls to clear a large floor space for dancing, and the growing crowd was soon elbow to elbow. The back door was opened to move the air, and small groups of men drifted out the door to nip whiskey from the flat flasks hidden in their coats.

At eight o'clock Chris the baker removed his violin from its frayed case. He hopped on a chair and held his bow high, calling out loudly over the din of the voices.

"And now may the dance begin!"

For the next three hours, young and old whirled about the room breathlessly with flushed, beaming faces. As it neared the hour of eleven, the party prepared to leave the dance and move up the street to the hotel where dinner waited, and St. Nicholas would soon appear to pass out gifts.

Coats were retrieved from the heaping pile, and mittens, scarves, hats and mufflers were located. The group passed noisily down the street, the cold snow squeaking underfoot and the air frosty.

Kate met them with a large pot of hot grog, filling the hotel with the enticing scent of the cloves. The long table in the dining room was laden with the many dishes brought in earlier by the guests; baked ham, roasted chickens, elk steaks, elk stew, mashed potatoes, corn bread, white rolls, biscuits and butter, sauerkraut, boiled cabbage, baked squash, roasted duck, beef tongue, smoked fish, pickled green beans, pickled beets, baked navy beans in brown sugar sauce, and fruit preserves of many varieties. The desserts were set in the kitchen for later.

The feast was greeted with hearty appreciation and growling stomachs. On the long plank table, Kate and Josie had spread a forest green linen tablecloth, and lit tall white candles in silver holders. These were placed at each end of the table, and a centerpiece of pine branches, red apples and oranges decorated the middle of the table.

Cumbersome coats and wraps were again discarded in a steaming heap in the corner of the parlor, and the guests settled themselves on the benches that had been brought up from the schoolhouse. The children waited anxiously for St. Nicholas' imminent arrival.

The tree was the center of attention, decorated with lit candles; each set in a tin dish and fastened to a furry, blue-green branch. Many small, colored glass balls hung by loops of heavy thread from the branches and a long chain of strung popcorn was draped about the tree. The glass ornaments twinkled and glistened from the candlelight. The sight brought a lump to Kate's throat for these ornaments had come from her grandmother's London home and had been part of her childhood Christmases.

Underneath the tree lay dozens of wrapped presents of all shapes and sizes. When the benches were full, the merry chatter of the group was interrupted by a deep voice booming out from behind the swinging pantry doors.

"Ho, Ho, Ho! Merry Christmas!"

The doors burst open, and out came St. Nicholas in a red flannel suit and tall black boots. His somewhat yellowed cotton beard masked the continuous train of "Ho, Ho, Ho's!" A large bulging burlap sack was flung over his shoulder as he lumbered toward the Christmas tree.

The children surrounded St. Nicholas, really Chris, at his seat of honor beside the tree. They presented him with a tray of gingerbread cookies and a steaming cup of grog. He reached into his sack and pulled out sticks of pink and white striped peppermint candy, one for each awestruck child who sat at his feet. Soon, they were quietly sucking on their sweet, sticky treats. The quiet ended when St. Nicholas started passing out the gifts from beneath the tree.

One of the older children carefully read the name off each gift and St. Nicholas handed it to that person. Each child received one gift, cloth dolls for the girls and knives for the boys, who immediately put them to use, whittling small sticks of wood from the kindling box. A mother or father gratefully accepted a new apron, a hat, or a perhaps a pair of gloves.

Eventually St. Nicholas reached the bottom of his pile of gifts. And to Josie's amazement, she heard her own name called out. On her lap, St.

Nicholas placed a heavy rectangular box, wrapped in paper and tied with a worn silk ribbon. The plain card bore her name in printed letters. The room grew quiet as everyone watched her unwrap the gift. Her slender fingers trembled slightly as she struggled with the knot in the ribbon. When at last she pushed back the paper and lifted the lid of the box, there lay a folded red cloth. Josie lifted the cloth, and then gasped in surprise at what lay beneath.

A beautiful pair of black dancing shoes, with shining silver heels rested on the cloth. Josie had never seen such lovely shoes. With the greatest of care, she lifted one shoe from the box and ran her fingers over the silver heels—the metal was cold. The black leather was stitched in perfect, tiny stitches. Up the ankle of the shoe were seven small shiny black buttons for fastening the shoes. And on the tip of each toe was a silver cap, no bigger than a thimble. Josie sat speechless with the shoe in her lap.

Kate appeared at her elbow and exclaimed "Josie, you must put them on and dance for us. We heard that you are quite a fine dancer!"

Josie looked up at her friend in surprise. "Why, who ever told you such a thing?"

Kate smiled at her and said, "A little bird told us you used to dance on the stage! We won't let you leave this room until we see at least one dance, Josie. You must! After all, it is Christmas."

Kate had both the shoes unbuttoned and was actually pulling Josie's shoes off her feet. She knelt on the floor in front of Josie and whispered, "Please, Josie! It would be such a treat for the children! Just one dance." She fastened the tiny black buttons around Josie's small ankles.

A man's voice interrupted and Josie looked up, startled.

"I had them made special for you, Josie. Are you ready to try them out?" It was Jack Herndon, and when Josie looked at him she felt her cheeks go hot. Her heart was beating rapidly, and she could not even speak. She looked at his extended hand. As if in a trance, Josie gave him her hand, and he guided her to her feet.

St. Nicholas picked up the violin and started the waltz. Round and round the room they danced, so fast that the candles on the tree and the kerosene lamps melted into a blur. Josie hardly felt her feet touch the wood plank floor. With one of his arms pressed snugly against Josie's back, Jack almost lifted her into the air as they waltzed in joyous circles around the hotel parlor. Other couples rose from their seats, and in minutes the room was filled with dancers.

St. Nicholas gave up his disguise and reappeared with his violin, ready now for some serious fiddling. The younger children were put down to sleep on the piles of coats near the warm wood stove. As their eyes closed, they still clutched their dolls and small knives.

Jack Herndon took several of the men over with him to the saloon and they returned with large buckets of foaming ale. Trays of cookies and several cakes were brought from the kitchen. Mugs were dipped out and passed around to the thirsty group. The buckets of ale were refilled again, and then the dancing continued and did not stop until the first hint of light—at about five a.m.

The sleeping children were bundled into blankets and placed into the wagons with hot stones wrapped in cloth to keep their feet warm for the long ride home. Good-byes and Merry Christmases were exchanged by all, as the groups departed one wagonload after another from the hotel. Everyone agreed that it had been a most wonderful party.

The people who lived in Buckskin Joe set off on foot toward their homes in the still dark morning, and Josie, Kate, Tommy and Samuel went off to their beds in the hotel. They were going to get a few hours of sleep before they cleared up the mess from the evening. And wait for Jack to discover his gift!

❦

On Christmas morning Jack awoke in his cabin after a few short hours of sleep. The freezing air was sharp in his nostrils as he lay still beneath the warm, heavy blankets. Because he had been gone all evening at the dance and the Christmas dinner at the hotel, no fire had been lit last night, making the cabin even colder than usual.

It was still and quiet at this early hour, and not a branch stirred on the great fir tree that grew beside Jack's cabin. His sleep-fogged mind began to sift slowly through the memories of the evening before—the dance at the schoolhouse and then the dinner and party at the hotel. He could picture Josie's sparkling, dark blue eyes as she smiled up at him while they danced round and round the hotel parlor. His heart beat harder at the memory of the warm touch of her hand and the feel of her body held close to his.

The laughter of the party still sounded faintly in his ears, and he could see the shining faces of excited children as they sat at St. Nicholas' knee waiting for their gifts. He still smelled the sharp piney scent of the freshly cut tree and the mouthwatering aroma of the roast meats mingling with the spicy smells of cinnamon and cloves from the grog kettle, which simmered all evening on the stove.

Because this was the biggest celebration of the year, almost all the townspeople would spend Christmas day in a slightly blurry state. Even the children would rise a bit later and more slowly than usual, with misty memories of the magical night before when St. Nicholas came to visit.

From his frosty window Jack could see the wispy curl of snow hovering motionless above the high mountain peaks to the west, like a frozen white wave. From so many miles away this was a telltale sign of the strong chill wind that was whipping off the highest peaks above Buckskin Joe.

Jack's cabin was set in a valley below the Mosquito Range, where it was sheltered from wind. Yellow rays of morning sunshine streamed through the woods, lighting the still pine boughs to a warm shade of green. Wind or no wind, one thing was certain—this Christmas day was very, very, cold—colder than usual for December 25th in Buckskin Joe.

Finally, at the risk of falling back to sleep again, Jack sat upright and began to dress himself as quickly as he could. Clad only in gray long johns he felt the cold air straight to his bones. By the time he had finished dressing and was heading out the door to begin his chores, the sky to the east showed a particularly beautiful sunrise of light pink clouds scattered high above the mountains.

Jack walked across the snowy yard toward the barn. The two dogs leaped around their master's legs, furiously wagging their tails. He stumbled over them and yelled, "Move it!" The dogs took no notice. Jack pushed open the heavy wooden barn door and heard the familiar nicker of greeting from Ty, who stood in the large stall. In the dim light of the interior he could just barely make out the outline of her head as he moved closer to pat her furry neck, thick with winter hair.

As his eyes slowly adjusted to the darkness of the barn, Jack could more easily see about him, and now the grain bin, feed buckets, pitchforks and shovels were visible. He lifted the large stone off the lid of the grain bin and propped the hinged cover against the wall. Then he scooped out a generous measure of oats with a can and went over to dump them into the feed trough that was nailed to the stall wall. As he looked over the log partition into the stall, he stopped in mid-action and stared. There, beside Ty in the dark barn, stood a red colt contentedly munching hay wisps from the rack.

Jack stood frozen, staring at the little red colt with the crooked white stripe running down his nose. Finally he set the can down, then climbed over the partition. He slowly swung down from the fence, taking care not to startle the colt. He moved between the two horses, talking quietly to them. Ty sniffed at his hands, then at his hair, blowing her warm breath on him. Then she nudged him with her muzzle, letting him know she was waiting for that grain that he had scooped out.

The colt seemed undisturbed by Jack's presence, and merely turned from the hayrack to look curiously at the newcomer for a moment. After this short inspection the colt resumed his rhythmic chewing.

Jack stepped closer to the colt and gently laid his hand upon its shoulder. The little horse flicked his ears in recognition of the touch, but continued to pull great mouthfuls of hay from the rack.

"You're a hungry one, aren't you boy?" said Jack, as he ran his hand lightly down the horse's side. "And a bit ribby, too! Where ever it was you came from, they sure didn't feed you so good, did they?" Then Jack saw the sign that was tacked up high on the stall wall. Large letters spelled out MERRY CHRISTMAS JACK! He recognized Tommy's handwriting. This horse was for him! Where had he come from? Who had gotten it? His mind was spinning with questions.

After visiting with the horses for quite a while, Jack eased himself over the log fence partition and prepared to leave the barn. He fussed with the horse supplies, checked the level of oats in the covered wooden bin, then decided to open another sack and fill the bin, which was almost empty. He cut open the burlap sack and dumped its contents into the bin, then took down the pitchfork and tidied up the open isle of the barn. He climbed the small ladder into the loft and speared several extra fork loads of hay from the stack and tossed them down to the horses. Jack was hesitant to let the new red colt from his sight, and he lingered sometime longer, leaning against the log rail fence watching the two horses eat their hay in the soft morning light.

❦

LATER THAT MORNING, over a stack of buckwheat pancakes in the hotel kitchen Jack learned that Josie, Tommy, Kate and Samuel had pooled their money together to buy him the red colt. He was more deeply touched than he had ever been before. Jack set down his fork and pressed his hands against the table, trying to collect himself as he blinked back tears when they told him how they'd sent Samuel off on a search for the horse. He enjoyed the story immensely.

Samuel explained how he had found the colt in Leadville at the livery stable where he frequently put the team up for the night. The colt had belonged to the notorious gambler Doc Holliday, the eccentric dentist who was better known for his abilities at the poker table than for the work he did on people's teeth.

Due to worsening symptoms from tuberculosis, Doc Holliday rarely left his hotel room in Leadville and had decided to sell the colt. He barely had enough strength to walk a block down the street, let alone train and ride a young horse. The owner of the Leadville livery stable agreed to trade a nice pistol for the young horse.

"Didn't Doc Holliday just die in Glenwood Springs?" asked Kate.

"Yes, he went down there just a few weeks ago for the healing waters, but it was too late. They say he was coughing up blood even before he left Leadville. He knew he was dying."

"I think I'll name him Doc Holliday," Jack said around a mouthful of pancakes. Tommy stuffed a whole slice of home-cured bacon in his mouth, and nodded in agreement. Kate refilled everyone's coffee up.

"It's a fine name, Jack," she said.

Josie, who'd kept silent all morning, glowed in happiness. Samuel reached for more buckwheat pancakes.

"Let's hope he's a better man than his namesake!"

NINE

NOT TOO LONG AFTER CHRISTMAS, news came to Buckskin Joe of a disastrous fire in Chicago, where many people had perished and hundreds more lost their homes and all their possessions. A local citizen who had family in Chicago organized a fund-raising event to collect relief money for the fire victims. Donations of useful items such as clothing and blankets were sought, as well as performers for the event. Jack offered use of the saloon for the evening and sales from beer would be added to the relief coffers.

Because of the charitable nature of the event, Josie agree to perform several dances for the audience. In the upstairs sitting room of the hotel she rehearsed the fancy steps, which she had learned so many years ago at the dance classes in St. Louis. Luckily, she had brought her costumes with her to Colorado, and they still fit.

For the performance, the front of the barroom was transformed into a stage. A wooden platform was draped with white cloth and all the tables were pushed back. In front of the stage area a large red curtain hung. When the evening came, a large group of townspeople filed through the saloon door and there was a great sense of hushed excitement as the rows of wooden benches, built just for this event, were quickly filled. A large can was passed around, and each family deposited a donation in it. Families that could not afford a cash donation brought items such as warm coats, hats, gloves, and thick woolen blankets.

Most of the clothing items and blankets were worn, but even the tiniest holes had been carefully repaired. Everyone contributed, no matter the sacrifice. Even some of the children placed a hard won coin or two in the money can.

In no time at all the benches were full, and the show was ready to begin. Kate turned down the wicks on all the lamps except two, which hung from the ceiling on wires to light the stage area. The audience grew quiet in anticipation of the show.

Slowly the heavy red curtains open. Tommy, acting as stagehand, opened them by grasping the bottom corner and crawling across the platform on his hands and knees.

In stage center, posed like a statue, was Josie, wearing a beautiful blue silk embroidered Chinese dress with short sleeves and a small-buttoned collar. The dress was tight fitting and from her small waist, a narrow skirt hung below her knees. Above her head she held a large, delicately painted fan. It covered part of her face. She had painted her face with white makeup and her lips deep red, with black lines around her eyelids curled upward to exaggerate the length of her eyelashes and transforming her into an exotic Chinese dragon goddess. Her dark hair was carefully arranged in a fancy, smooth roll on the back of her head, and several large golden hair ornaments were set into the bun. On her feet were the new silver-heeled dancing shoes.

She was poised with one heel up and one hand on her waist.

Some of the people in the audience gasped audibly. For a long minute or two Josie kept her eyes fixed on some point high on the saloon ceiling. Only the dangling decorations from the golden hair ornament trembled slightly as she stood motionless in her pose.

From somewhere behind the bar a solitary fiddle started to play, and Josie snapped her fan shut and began to dance. She floated across the platform in perfect time to the enchanting Oriental music, her hands moving intricately through the air as she performed. Then she snapped the painted fan open, and used the prop as if it were her partner. The strange and beautiful dance ended with Josie holding her starting pose, with the fan held above her head.

The curtain closed jerkily across the platform, pulled by the unseen hand of Tommy. Thunderous applause rose from the audience, leaving no doubt of their approval of Josie's performance. Jack rose from his seat in the second row as he clapped. How beautiful and exotic Josie looked! He could not wait to see her after the dance—alone! Jack felt as if he might burst from anticipation.

After a short intermission, the curtain opened again. This time Josie was dressed as a Spanish dancer, in a low-cut brilliant yellow dress that revealed her shoulders. The full skirt hung nearly to her ankles, and peaking beneath were yards and yards of black ruffled petticoat with white edging. For this dance her hair was pinned in a pile of large soft curls and crowned with a long mantilla. Her cheeks were rouged and her eyelids painted blue. On one cheek a black spot was painted.

The fiddle music started again, and Josie began a lively Spanish dance with quick stomping of her silver shoes upon the stage and many lively flourishes with her ruffled petticoat. How excited she was to be dancing on stage again! She threw herself totally into the moment. The quick pace of the music was contagious, and the audience began to clap and shout along. When the song ended with a great shout of "Ole!" Josie held her great skirt in her hands and curtsied low, her head bowed to the crowd.

The applause was deafening, punctuated with ear-splitting wolf whistles from Tommy. Someone from the audience shouted "Silverheels, Silverheels!" The entire group took up the chant. All this commotion riled up the dogs in attendance, and they added their excited barking to the atmosphere.

Several minutes later, Josie emerged from the back room, which had served as her dressing room. She was dressed in her regular clothes, and her face was still quite flushed. Never had Josie felt more radiant. Immediately she was surrounded by a group of excited friends who wished to share their congratulations.

"Josie! You were wonderful!" Kate said. "I wish you could have seen yourself as we did. It was just beautiful!" Kate hugged her friend tightly with tears sparkling in the corners of her eyes. "You should be on the stage in London or New York, not hidden here in this mining town!"

Josie kissed Kate on the cheek and laughed merrily.

"Thank you, Kate! I'm not sure I'm ready for the big city yet, though. I better have a bit more practice!"

Jack hugged her spontaneously. "It was great, Josie! You were incredible!"

"Josie, that was the best dancing I've ever seen!" said Tommy excitedly. "You'll have to do another show real soon!"

Josie ruffled Tommy's hair. "Thank you, Tommy. That's something for me to think about!"

Jack took Josie's hand.

"Josie, Chris is setting up to play his fiddle right now. We've moved the benches. May I have the honor of the first dance?"

Josie kept hold of his hand, "Why, there's no one in the world I'd rather dance with than you, Jack!"

Then, to the accompaniment of Turkey in the Straw, the two whirled their way around the wide saloon floor, encouraging several other couples to join them. Josie's dark eyes sparkled in the softly lit room with an intensity Jack had never seen before. As he held her close and spun her round in the fast reel, he felt a deep pride that this beautiful woman cared for him. He pulled her close and whispered in her ear, "Marry me, Silverheels." Josie wasn't sure she'd heard Jack right, but the next song had started, and she was pulled onto the dance floor by Tommy.

The fact that Tommy had never danced didn't really matter, and the two hopped and skipped about the floor. After a few turns around the room they were laughing so hard they almost fell over.

Josie was the belle of the ball and each man vied for a dance with her. She longed to dance with Jack again, and tried to catch his eye across the crowded room. Finally, Jack broke into a dance with Samuel and she was in his arms again.

The floor was getting crowded now. Right there in the middle of the room, Jack kissed Josie on the lips. A cheer went up from the people around them, and Josie pulled away with pleasure and embarrassment as they clapped.

Jack leaned close and whispered in her ear, "I love you, Silverheels."

She smiled at him and didn't have a moment to answer before Chris began playing Devil's Dream, and the dancing again took off at a fast clip. The dancing did not subside until the wee hours. The evening was a success all around.

It seemed that winter was settling in for good. Very few sunny days interrupted the succession of storms that rolled across the high country of Colorado.

Pastimes such as skiing were rapidly growing in popularity. In Buckskin Joe, a women's club had just formed, and every Saturday afternoon the ladies met for an exhilarating few hours of skiing in the open meadows above Buckskin Joe.

As the month of January drew to a close, everything seemed all right with the world. The people of the town socialized more, enjoying sleigh rides, snowshoeing parties, and late night dances. These activities built friendships that had little chance to develop during busier times.

In the first week of February, Samuel made a routine stop at Buena Vista, about thirty miles south of Buckskin Joe. Waiting for a ride up to Buckskin Joe were three Mexicans. They were traveling north from New Mexico territory to the gold fields of high Colorado. They tossed their blanket rolls atop the pile of luggage already tied to the rack and climbed aboard the stage. The apparent leader of the ragged group did most of the talking, in broken English.

"We make the money of the gold mine," he said to Samuel as they drove up the steep incline of Trout Creek Pass out of Buena Vista. "We weel come back for our wives and cheeldren in Mexico, where they wait for us." His wide grin displayed several gaps between large, stained teeth. His optimism was apparent however, for his dark brown eyes were alight with hope.

"We shall be reech weeth the gold!"

The other men who sat behind them on top of the stage cabin nodded furiously in agreement.

"Si, Si, get reech!"

Samuel enjoyed his new travel acquaintances. After a while he began to understand the cadence of their speech and listened to the stories of their homes and travels. As the gradual decent into the long wide stretch of the great South Park began, Jorge, the leader, sighed.

"Que bueno!"

He spent the next ten miles telling Samuel about his wife and three young children who were living in Mexico. A large herd of elk, several hundred head easily, grazed about a half-mile from the stage.

Samuel told his passengers about the great variety of wild game which was hunted in the area, from deer to moose to bear, buffalo, and elk.

"Most of the meat we eat up here is wild game," he said. "A few people have cattle ranches, but beef is expensive, while wild game is plentiful. Most of the people who keep cows or chickens do it for the milk and eggs, not for the meat."

He told them of the Ute Indians who had settled the plains before the white man came, and of their anger over the intrusion and the building of fences across the open lands.

"There were some uprisings, and now the Ute are being steadily pushed out of their great hunting grounds." Samuel shook his head as he continued, "I can't say as I blame them for being angry over the loss of their land, but it doesn't do them much good when they go and kill a few ranchers. They get driven farther out by even angrier groups of whites."

Samuel's face grew somber as he said, "They really don't have a fighting chance to keep their land. The worst thing for them is the disease that the white men bring. The Indians are defenseless against them, and die by the hundreds. Whole tribes are almost completely wiped out, and those who are left are so weakened they just keep retreating further and further from the white man's settlements." He shook his head, and said, "It's a sad thing to witness, the vanishing of their way of life. I have a great respect for Indians. In many ways they are living better lives than the white man."

For several moments, all that was heard was the clopping of hooves on the frozen dirt and the rhythmic squeaking of the stagecoach springs.

"Well, no one said that life was fair, did they?" said Samuel. Little did he know how prophetic these words would be.

∽

THE STAGE DREW NEAR to Fairplay just as the full moon began to rise above the eastern horizon, casting an orange hue over the dark sky and the clouds clustered near the mountains. Samuel always enjoyed driving under the light of the full moon, for the light that was cast made it nearly as bright as day. As they passed by Buffalo Peaks, there was already enough light to make out the distinguishing features of the ridge for which the peaks owed their name. Samuel pointed out the peaks and the Mexicans made appreciative sounds.

As the light of the moon reflected off of the flat stretch of prairie and the snowy mountain peaks, which rimmed the great South Park, Samuel's excitement grew over seeing Kate again. The stage rolled steadily along, it ate up the five miles between Fairplay and Alma. On the final three-mile ascent to Buckskin Joe, Samuel kept up a lively conversation with his Mexican passengers.

He told them about the town's businesses: the mercantile, the bakery, and the saloon. He told them about the mines and mentioned some people they should look up the next morning to ask about work. In anticipation of seeing Kate, he spoke glowingly of her wonderful cooking at the hotel and the clean and comfortable lodgings available there. The three Mexicans listened carefully to the information, punctuating his conversation with "Si, Si, senor's."

When Samuel finally pulled the tired and steaming team to a halt in front of the hotel, he called out merrily.

"Here we are!"

His announcement was intended as much for those inside the hotel as for his passengers.

The door of the hotel swung open.

"Samuel, Samuel!" Kate's excited voice rang out, as her quick steps took her down the wooden porch steps toward him. Almost before her feet had touched the snow, she flung her arms about his neck and covered his prickly cheek with kisses.

He gathered her up in his big arms and buried his face in her soft curly hair. "I missed you Kate!" he whispered into her ear before he kissed her. The passengers watched with amusement.

THE NEW DAWN BROKE as clear as a bell. The sky was a sapphire blue over the white mountain peaks. Not a whisper of wind stirred the treetops which were visible from the hotel windows. Floating up the stairwell were the delicious smells of frying bacon and brewing coffee. Kate never needed to use a dinner bell to call her guests to the breakfast table; the mouthwatering aromas that came from the kitchen were announcement enough.

Kate was up even earlier than usual due to her excitement over Samuel's presence. And this morning her heart was not heavy with the dread of him leaving because last night he had told her that he would be able to stay over for two nights—just to be with her!

She stood with her back toward the kitchen door and stirred a large bowl of buckwheat pancake batter for breakfast. Because of the extra guests from the stage there would need to be even more food than usual today. Kate gave a small shriek of surprise as a pair of large, strong hands grasped her about the waist. With a dripping batter spoon still in her hand, she turned to face Samuel.

"You scared me half to death!" she said with feigned annoyance. "Now look at the mess I've made!" Small drops of batter made a trail of tiny white circles on the floorboards, as he kissed her.

Samuel kissed her anyway, "It sure is good to be back here with you again, Kate."

A loud knocking upon the back door of the hotel interrupted their quiet moment together. Kate looked at Samuel in surprise.

"Come in!"

Jack Herndon appeared at the kitchen door, looking disheveled and not wearing a coat or hat even at such a chill hour of the morning. Although he was winded from having run over to the hotel, he immediately burst out with his news.

"It's those three Mexicans who came on the stage. They're very sick! They can't even take water. We need a doctor!"

Jack wiped his hand across his brow. "I found them burning up with the fever. They aren't making sense. One of them keeps screaming, "Maria! Maria!" That's how I knew something was wrong. I could hear the screams from the bar when I was sweeping up this morning."

Samuel was in his coat and hat and already at the door when he said, "I'll ride to Fairplay and fetch the doctor. I'll be back as soon as I can."

Kate sprang into action just as quickly, gathering the supplies she would need for doctoring the sick men: several old sheets, a bottle of whiskey, and a packet of tea were thrown into a basket.

Tommy stood in the back doorway of the kitchen, still in his gray woolen underwear with his hair sticking up at odd angles. He had been deep in a dream about a hotel with its dining room full of travelers. The people kept calling for food no matter how fast he ran with the trays. When he woke with a start, he realized that the voices he heard were not part of his dream. It was Kate and Samuel and Jack talking loudly in the kitchen. From the worried sound of their voices and the quick footsteps and banging doors, he knew something must be wrong.

Before she hurried out the door, Kate noticed him. "Tommy! Ask Josie to finish serving breakfast, then have her come to the bunkhouse at the saloon. Those men who arrived with Samuel last night have taken sick. Samuel's already fetching the doctor."

Without waiting for an answer, Kate ran out the door.

Jack was holding the door for her when she entered the dark bunkhouse behind the saloon. She drew in her breath sharply at the thick smell of illness. The men lay on pallets.

"Oh my Lord!" she said with a shaky voice.

Kneeling down, she placed her hand on one man's forehead. He lay on his back while his feverish eyes stared blankly at the ceiling. His breathing was shallow and labored, his lips cracked and bleeding.

Kate called to Jack, "We've got to cool them down quickly!"

She felt the foreheads of the other two men and shook her head.

"They're all just as bad. Let's try to cool them down with snow packs. Fill some socks with snow, and I'll put them against their bodies."

Jack nodded and ran to fetch some of his socks.

When he returned, Kate directed him to fill each sock with snow from the nearby snow bank. They knotted the socks and placed them underneath the men's clothing against their skin.

Kate said, "Let's sponge them off with water now; it will help to cool them."

Kate ripped the sheets into strips, and when Jack returned from the saloon with a basin of cold water, the two laid wet rags on each man's forehead and wiped their hot bodies with cool water.

Aside from an occasional moan, not a sound passed the men's cracked lips as Kate and Jack worked grimly side-by-side. The smallest of the men, nearest the bunkhouse wall, seemed to be the worst. His raspy breathing was ragged and labored and his swollen eyes were closed.

Kate replaced the cold, wet rags time and time again, but the man's skin remained hot to the touch.

She said, "I hope the doctor comes soon. I fear for these poor men."

Jack steadily wiped the arms of one man with his cold, wet cloth. "Samuel should be on his way back by now. Let's just hope he found the doctor at home!"

When Samuel finally ran into the bunkhouse nearly a half an hour later, his face was dripping with sweat from the hard ride.

"The doctor's not coming! He went to Nebraska to visit. Won't be back for a few weeks." He glanced at the men. "How are they doing?"

Kate shook her head in despair. "Not good, Samuel. We need a doctor and now! I'm at a loss for what to do."

Jack Herndon's voice became hushed. "I'm afraid this poor fellow has left us. God bless his soul." He bowed his head in respect for the dead man. "He came all that way from Mexico and never had a chance to see his dreams unfold. It just isn't fair." He sighed. "Samuel, we had best lay him out in the barn."

Samuel stood by the door with his coat still on and his hat in his hand. He stepped over to Kate and rested his hand on her shoulder. Tears glistened on her cheeks as she looked up at him. He leaned down and gently kissed her before helping Jack remove the body.

The two men went about their somber business while Kate stayed with the remaining men. Soon after Jack and Samuel left, Josie and Tommy came to the door.

"Don't come in! I think they have smallpox!" Kate said through a crack in the door.

"They're bad off, no doubt. One has died already. Jack and Samuel took him out to the barn."

This news shocked the two newcomers speechless.

Kate continued, glumly, "Dr. Richards has gone to Nebraska for two weeks, so there goes that hope." She shook her head. "I've no idea how to help these men."

Tommy stood by the door as if frozen to the spot, but Josie hurried inside.

"Don't worry, Kate. You rest now. I'll tend to these men for a while, and Tommy will help. Go on outside and breathe some fresh air for a bit. I'm sure we'll soon find a doctor, but in the meantime we'll do the best we can for these poor souls."

Despite Kate's tired protests, Josie escorted her to the door and gently pushed her into the sunlight. Then Josie took over where Kate left off.

The men did not improve by the end of that long day. Near midnight, a second man died, and the third man looked very close to death, too.

By now, like the others, his face was covered with angry red spots, and the rash grew with each passing hour. Bumps began appearing upon his chest and arms, and his breathing became weaker.

The small group that attended to this last survivor was exhausted by sundown of the second day. Kate, Josie, and Jack took turns sitting with the sick man, so there would be a little sleep for everyone. In spite of these breaks, sleep was fitful. Samuel had gone to Como looking for another doctor. When he returned at midnight—without a doctor—a wan group was waiting for him.

"Too late, anyway," Jack said, wearily. "Last one died this afternoon. He was a pitiful sight."

After putting the horses up in the barn, Samuel joined the others who sat slumped around the kitchen table.

"I can't believe how fast they went! What kind of fever does that? I just don't know what to make of it." He felt more tired than he'd ever felt.

Kate put her arm around his shoulders and leaned her head against his. "We all did the best we could, Lord knows. Luck was against us that no doctors could come to help, but we did all we could for those men, Samuel. I know that God knows our effort, and now they are safe with Him."

Her eyes filled with tears and her voice became choked with emotion as she continued. "It just pains me to think of their families back in Mexico waiting to hear from them. We don't even know who they are or how to send word to their loved ones that their men have died!" Tears brimmed from her reddened eyes and rolled down her cheeks as she spoke, and Kate reached for the dishcloth to wipe her eyes.

"All we found was this picture in the pocket of one of their coats," said Josie, pointing to a small, worn picture of a young Hispanic woman wearing a large striped shawl covering most of her black dress. Her hair was tightly braided and hung down in two long plaits. She was seated on a wooden box and behind her, one could make out the fuzzy horizon of a plowed field. The young woman barely smiled and couldn't have been much more than fifteen years old.

"There are no names written anywhere and no papers with their belongings. All they had were the clothes on their backs and their bedrolls." Josie touched the edge of the picture. "And this."

"How about some tea?" Kate asked.

The group thought about Mexico, and family, and lost dreams, as Kate filled the kettle with water. The rhythmic ticking of the clock and the crackling of the fire were the only other sounds.

When the kettle whistled, Kate gathered four large cups from the kitchen shelf and put them on a tray. She also brought a flask of whiskey to the table, and added a good measure of the liquor to each cup.

"A bit of whiskey never hurt anyone, and I could use a good night's sleep tonight," she said, as she sat back down. "I like mine with honey." She felt more tired than she'd ever felt, as she stirred a spoonful of thick, golden honey into her tea.

They sipped their tea and talked in quiet voices so as not to wake Tommy in his bunk behind the pantry. The whiskey soothed their nerves and relaxed their minds. When the clock's hands were pushing toward one o'clock, they made their way to their respective rooms to sleep.

❧

THE NEXT MORNING, shortly after dawn, someone banged hard on the hotel door. Kate awoke with difficulty, still sluggish from a deep sleep. She stumbled downstairs, her nightgown strangely damp. On the doorstep stood Liza Jenkins, a neighbor girl with yellow braids. She wore no hat, and her coat was opened to the frigid temperature, revealing a thin dress beneath. She was obviously distraught.

Kate beckoned her to come in, and the girl rushed into her open arms, crying.

"It's Ma and Pa! They're frightful sick! They've got the fever and red spots all over their faces! You've got to come help me, Miss Kate! You've got to come quick!"

"Now, don't panic, Liza, I'll— "All of a sudden, Kate's heart started beating fast and her head began to pound in pain. Red flashed before her eyes, and she reached out to Liza in confusion. One second later, Kate was on the floor unconscious.

Liza Jenkins began to shriek.

When Josie ran down the stairs, she found Kate in a heap on the floor. After quieting Liza, she sent Tommy to fetch Jack, who returned within moments with Samuel by his side. The two men, in their sleeping flannels and boots, carried Kate to her bed upstairs. To everyone's horror Kate was displaying symptoms similar to the dead men. Fear filled Josie's heart as she saw Kate's dangling head draped over Samuel's arm.

"Josie, my Ma and Pa are sick! Someone must come quickly!"

Josie looked at Liza's tear-streaked face, and took pity on her. "Let me get dressed, then Jack and I will go with you."

Josie threw on some clothes and the trio set off up the hill to tend to Liza's folks. When they arrived, Liza took her young brother, who'd been watching their sick parents and baby sister, into the other room. Josie wondered how long they would have parents, as she looked at another set of feverish faces.

Jack, Josie, Tommy and Samuel spent another exhausting day, this time attending two stricken households. Jack closed the hotel and dining room, until he could figure out who would do what. On top of caring for the sick, the chores still needed tending, and Jack and Tommy shared those. Samuel decided to set off for Trout Creek Pass and Buena Vista in hopes of finding a doctor who would come. It wouldn't be easy convincing someone to come right away. Josie went back and forth between the hotel and the Jenkins home, caring for everyone.

Shortly after Samuel left town, Josie regretted his going, for it seemed Jack was falling ill, too. His face had gone pale and he was soaked with sweat. As Josie held cold rags to his forehead, his hands were shaking badly.

After putting Jack to bed in her own room, Josie was very near to collapse herself. She was exhausted and worried and she knew what she had to do. Grabbing Tommy, she led him to the kitchen table and pulled him down to his knees.

"Josie, what are we doing?" His voice quivered, and Josie realized he was near to breaking down.

"We're going to pray, Tommy. God is our only hope."

They knelt on the wooden floor of the hotel kitchen with their heads bowed against the bench, their hands clasped tightly in their laps. Tommy had never been much of a churchgoer but he followed Josie's lead.

"Dear God," Josie whispered. "Please, heal these good people from this sickness, and protect them with Your love. And send us a doctor," Josie tried to take the commanding tone out of her voice, "if You please, that is. Amen."

Josie sat with her eyes closed, while Tommy echoed her "Amen." The two of them remained on their knees for several minutes in the darkened kitchen, hoping God had heard their pleas.

"When do you s'pose Samuel will make it back with a doctor? I sure wish they would hurry!" Tommy could not hide his fear any more. Jack and Kate had been his only family; he could not bear to think of either one actually dying. Who'd take care of him?

Ever since his father had left town without him, Kate and Jack had shown him love and kindness, the first he had ever known in his short life. There was nothing that Tommy wouldn't do to help them get better. He looked at Josie. Even pray.

Josie reached out and took the boy's hand. "It's a good day's ride each way, and we don't know if he'll find a doctor, but Samuel will be here as fast as he can." She wanted to ease the worried look on Tommy's face, but given the circumstances, it would be kinder not to pretend everything will be fine. Josie had learned from Kate that life was tough in the mountains. Best to accept it. Still, she doubted that would be a comfort if her beloved Jack didn't get better.

The next three days were an endless nightmare for Josie. Getting only sporadic periods of fitful rest between long sessions of tending to the sick, she felt little better than death herself. She often felt dizzy, and her mind seemed foggy and unreal. She chalked it up to lack of sleep and worry over Jack and Kate.

Samuel had not returned, and no news of his progress had been sent the town's way. By this time word had gotten out that Buckskin Joe had been hit by an epidemic of the deadly smallpox. Terrified settlers from nearby mining towns dared not go to the town's aide, so great were their fears of contracting the awful disease.

Josie had read somewhere that smallpox, with its telltale rash of scarring eruptions, was known to cause blindness as well as death. She wished she could skip town like some inhabitants of Buckskin Joe who had hastily left under cover of darkness. But she couldn't leave her friends.

There was little more that Josie could do for the sick than give them sips of strong broth or tea for they were unable to keep any food down. If they kept liquids down, she sent a prayer of thanksgiving heavenward.

Jack was the worst; he was no longer able to take liquids. Josie sat by his bedside, replacing cool, wet cloths on his forehead for endless hours. She held his burning hand and tried not to weep. By the third night of his taking ill, Jack Herndon was barely clinging to life.

Josie knelt by the bed—her bed—where he lay motionless, whispering prayers and talking to the man she loved so dearly. This evening, Jack's shallow breathing had become fainter. Josie's heart twisted in pain at his suffering. Fearing the time was nearing when he would hear her no more, she tried once again to reach him.

"Jack. Dearest." She fought to keep the desperation from her voice.

Miraculously, Jack's eyes flickered open. "Josie," he whispered through cracked lips.

He tried to lift his head, but Josie laid her hand on his forehead.

"Rest, my love. I'm here."

She moved so she could look into his eyes. "I love you, Jack, and I'm proud that you love me. If I live through this epidemic, I will carry your love with me wherever I go."

"I love you too, Josie." With calm eyes, he looked up into her face. "I'll miss you."

Josie was crying silently. Her heart felt leaden.

"Hold me?" Jack's breath was slowing down.

Josie carefully climbed onto the bed and cradled Jack in her arms like a child. She whispered his name over and over, until she felt life leave him.

Darkness had fallen on Buckskin Joe, and the walls in the room were shadowed. Lying next to Jack, Josie felt peaceful. Holding him tightly in her arms, Josie slipped into sleep, the first and last time she would lie in a bed with Jack Herndon.

TEN

IT WAS FOUR DAYS after he left that Samuel finally returned to Buckskin Joe, and this time he brought a doctor. He had ridden all the way to the town of St. Elmo to find him, for the doctor had been called out of Buena Vista for a difficult birthing. The trip had been hard and slow up to St. Elmo, through the snowy high country of the Arkansas River Valley.

When Samuel and the doctor rode into Buckskin Joe they found it eerily quiet. No smoke curled from the chimneys of the houses as it usually did, and not a soul was to be seen walking down Main Street. They hurriedly hitched their horses by the hotel, and when Samuel opened the front door all was quiet, except for the hungry mews of a large, calico cat. Then, to his horror, he smelled that unmistakable stench of death.

He went into the kitchen and found soiled rags, tin cups, and pots of water scattered haphazardly about the table and counter of Kate's usually tidy kitchen.

"Oh my God!" cried Samuel.

He ran up the stairs, taking two at a time, toward Kate's bedroom. The door was ajar, and he pushed it open. He felt an immense flood of relief when he saw her lying there under the quilts, which rose and fell steadily with her breathing. With his heart still pounding from fear, Samuel sat down on the edge of Kate's bed. He laid his hand on her cheek.

"Kate, can you hear me? It's Samuel. I've brought a doctor back with me."

Kate moaned softly in her sleep but did not awaken.

Samuel was still sitting quietly on the edge of her bed when the tall, balding doctor appeared at the doorway.

"Mr. Grey, I'm afraid I've got some bad news. I've just found a man and a woman in the next room. It looks like the man died not too long ago, and the lady is ill with smallpox."

The doctor held his large black hat in his hands.

"It sure is a shame, fine looking young fellow he was. I hope we can pull his young wife through. It may be too late already." He sighed heavily, and shook his head. "It always pains me to be too late to help. But sometimes, that's just God's way, isn't it?" He looked at Samuel thoughtfully for a moment, and then walked over beside the bed where Kate lay. "Is this your gal, then?" he asked.

Samuel nodded, shocked about Jack's death.

The doctor became business-like and opened his bag, taking out medical items that he placed on the bedside table. Samuel stepped aside and watched while the doctor examined Kate.

When he was finished, he looked at Samuel. "She's got a good chance of coming through this. Her fever is on the way down from the looks of things. That's a very good sign, and the risk of blindness is very slight in such cases."

Samuel stiffened at these words.

"Try to get her to drink some water. Dehydration is the worst killer of all, regardless of the disease." The doctor clapped Samuel on the shoulder. "My guess is that your gal will be fine." His face grew somber. "The lady in the next room may not be so lucky. I'd best get right to work."

Samuel watched the doctor leave and then looked at Kate's handsome face. He was deeply relieved that her condition was hopeful and grateful for the doctor's help. His thoughts whirled about his tired mind. All those hours and miles he had ridden alone across the Colorado passes and plains to find a doctor his determination had never wavered. Now that he was back, reality seemed to be unraveling.

DURING HIS WELL-TRAVELED LIFE Samuel had seen many beautiful things—sunrises over the mountain peaks which tinged the snow from pink to gold, vast herds of elk and antelope that covered prairies end to end, pointed-ear mountain lions with their cubs, hunting mice by the edge of a forest. He'd also witnessed horrible things—senseless shootings, bloody scalpings, and the ravages of disease and starvation.

Of all the death he'd encountered, Jack's death hit him the hardest. He'd had everything, a thriving business, many friends, and a good woman. Although he knew he must, Samuel could not will his feet to walk through that door. Not yet, anyway.

Samuel began to cry.

The doctor appeared, his collar unbuttoned and his white sleeves rolled above his elbows. He looked with compassion at Samuel, understanding the process of grief. He walked over beside the bed and placed his hand on Samuel's arm.

"It would be best, Mr. Grey, if we were to take the body away. He must be separated from the living to protect them."

Samuel sniffed loudly and squared his shoulders. "It's not right. Jack

Herndon was a good man. The best kind of man." He wiped his tears with the back of his hand. "It would be an honor to carry his body out."

"Ready?" the doctor asked.

Samuel led the way.

Josie's labored breathing filled the room.

"Hello, young'un. You hang on there, okay?" Samuel caressed a wisp of hair from her brow. "There are people wanting to see you again."

Samuel noticed how peaceful Jack's face was as they covered it with the quilt. He was always amazed at how different a body felt when life was gone.

The trip down the narrow, steep stairway was like a funeral procession, the barn an unwilling tomb. The other bodies lay on boards spanning hastily constructed sawhorses. Jack was placed next to them. The bodies would keep frozen in the frigid air.

The doctor left, giving Samuel a moment of privacy. Samuel dragged a keg of nails to his friend's side and sat down. Ty and Doc Holliday trotted into the barn from the corral, neighing hungrily. Samuel got up and pitched some hay to them, and wondered if Jack's dogs had been fed recently. He'd check after he said goodbye to Jack.

THIS IS WHERE JACK had truly loved to be the most, spending hours puttering in the barn surrounded by his horses and dogs and the good earthy smell of dust, manure, and hay. And now he lay wrapped in a quilt on some old boards.

Samuel sat in the barn for some time, listening to the horses munching their hay. Memories of his friend played in his mind, as the color left the sky and the gray of twilight seeped into the woods behind the barn. Eventually he got up, patted the horses' behinds, and walked out of the barn. Before he swung the big door closed, he whispered into the darkness.

"Goodbye, old friend."

When all was said and done, nine people died from the smallpox in Buckskin Joe that spring. The doctor had stayed for over a week tending to the sick, before he packed his bag and mounted his horse to head back to St. Elmo. Samuel hitched up the team of bays to the stagecoach for the first time in over two weeks and drove along with the doctor as far as Buena Vista. He would stop to purchase much-needed supplies to take back to Buckskin Joe.

The two men shook hands at the juncture in the road that led to St. Elmo.

"Don't know how to thank you enough, doctor," said Samuel. "If you hadn't come, we surely would have lost many more folks. Buckskin Joe will always be in your debt."

"I'm glad to have helped, Mr. Grey. I've done all I can for them. What they need now is rest and time to heal." The doctor tipped the brim of his hat and then mounted his horse. "It's been a pleasure meeting you, Samuel." Then he shook the reins and headed south.

In addition to the three Mexican men and Jack, two children from the Barker family had died. Last to go were three miners who had been wintering in a small shack on the outskirts of town. Fortunately, the Jenkins children still had their parents.

Because the ground was frozen two feet down, it would be impossible to dig graves for some months. The bodies had been carefully wrapped in burlap and packed with salt and charcoal to preserve them. Placed in an old shed until spring thaw, they would be buried in the graveyard under the tall pines on the hill behind town.

Kate was slowly beginning to feel like herself again, but had lost a good deal of weight during her illness. The rosy bloom was gone from her cheeks. Just during the last several days she had felt strong enough to get up from her bed and station herself in a large rocking chair in the kitchen with quilts tucked about her as she sat close to the warm cast iron cook stove.

The fire snapped and crackled cheerfully, as her cats wound themselves about her ankles vying for the seat of choice in her lap. Absently she stroked Henry, the gray tiger's head, as he purred robustly. Once again, the cats were receiving attention.

After Kate's illness, the familiar surroundings of the kitchen seemed strange, out of kilter. With Jack gone, nothing would be the same again. Still, the bright sunlight streamed through the window and illuminated the kitchen with its cheerful liquid amber, and the clock still ticked its familiar rhythm. She wondered if life would take up its own familiar cadence sometime soon. We shall see, she thought. We shall see.

Samuel had left early that morning with the doctor, to bring back supplies. Josie was too ill to leave her bed, but the doctor had assured her she was out of danger. Nasty scars from the smallpox were forming all over her face, marring her beauty forever. But the fever had subsided, thank God.

Every half hour or so, Tommy came by the kitchen and checked on Kate, making sure she was warm enough, asking her if she was hungry.

His anxious attention made Kate's heart glow, and a few times when he came in she pretended to want tea, just to enjoy Tommy's company. When he'd brought her a second cup that morning, Kate ruffled his hair.

"Why Tommy, I declare, you run this kitchen better than I ever did! I've been hearing wonderful things about your elk stew. Seems you're going to put me out of a job!"

Tommy grinned at her praise. "Oh, I don't think so, Kate. Everyone's missed your cooking. They're pretty tired of eating nothing but elk stew every day. And boiled beans," Tommy said, as he left the room.

Kate laughed as she stirred a spoonful of honey into her cup.
It would feel good to get back to cooking for the hotel. In his will, Jack had left the hotel to her. Apparently he'd known how much she loved it.

Although she was finally able to be up and about, Kate was still weak and unable to help care for Josie. Every afternoon Kate sat with her and talked to her, trying to elicit a response from her friend.

When she was awake, Josie would look dully at the ceiling. Most of the time she slept, occasionally tossing and turning with troubled dreams. Sometimes she would cry out, and Kate would soothe her with soft words.

Kate did not tell Josie about Jack for she feared the news of his death would endanger her recovery. And it would be weeks before she'd hand Josie a mirror.

It was Josie, herself, who'd first brought up Jack's name. Lying in bed shortly after her fever broke, she'd finally turned to Kate with clear eyes.

"Jack. He's gone, isn't he?"

Kate squeezed her hand. "He passed on, Josie, the very same night you came down with the fever. The doctor said he died peacefully in your arms." Tears flowed down Kate's cheeks.

Josie reached out and trailed her finger through a tear. "You didn't get a chance to say goodbye, did you, Kate?" Then she looked upward, her eyes dull once more.

Kate sobbed on her friend's quilt. "I miss Jack, too."

Eventually Kate was feeling well enough to work in the kitchen again. By this time Josie had gained enough strength to sit in the kitchen for a few hours each day. Josie rarely responded to Kate's bright stream of chatter. After a few days, Kate gave up trying. They'd pass the hours quietly with Josie rocking slowly in the chair beside the warm stove while Kate cooked.

Kate worried most about the dull, lifeless look in Josie's eyes. She showed no interest in the world around her. She had turned inward, and Kate wondered if she would ever come back.

One morning Kate was up early preparing breakfast. Although there were few people to cook for, she enjoyed getting back to her regular routine again. The stage was coming through tonight, so Kate began peeling a large pan of potatoes for dinner. There might be a fair number of passengers, now that the smallpox scare was over. Kate was planning a dinner of fried potatoes with onions and salt pork, and for dessert, apple pie. When he was done with his morning chores, Tommy came and helped her slice the apples for the pies.

When the cooking was done, Kate looked up at the clock. "My goodness, it is half past nine! Josie is certainly sleeping late today." She wiped her hands on her apron. "Perhaps I should check on her. It's not like her to sleep this late."

The bedroom door was closed, so Kate knocked on it softly, calling Josie's name. There was no response. Feeling concerned by this time, Kate opened the door a few inches and peered in.

"Josie?"

Josie was not there. The sun streamed through the window, bright rays striking the neatly made bed. The pillows looked like they'd not been slept on and the quilt was pulled tight. Kate ran to the wardrobe and flung the doors open. It was empty. In disbelief, Kate searched the room, hoping to find a clue or a note about where her friend had gone.

But there was nothing except for a silver brooch shaped like a rosebud that had been carefully wrapped inside a handkerchief and left on the small dressing table. Kate picked up the brooch, feeling the cool metal in her hand. It was very ornate and appeared to be quite old. She had never seen it before.

Kate stood for some time, holding the brooch and thinking of her friend. She could hear the ticking of the hall clock and could smell the aroma of apple pies baking in the kitchen. A breeze from the opened window stirred the white lace curtains in Josie's bedroom. The breeze carried the fresh smell of spring and melting snow from the puddles that were already forming along the roadside.

That evening a large group of townspeople met in the hotel saloon to mull over Josie Pye's sudden disappearance. All afternoon they had searched, hoping to find her, thinking she may have taken ill again and wandered off. Not a nook or cranny was missed, for the townspeople had loved Josie. The children remembered her kindnesses; the Jenkins' reminded everyone how Josie had helped them through their bouts of smallpox; and Chris, the baker, reminisced about her beautiful dancing. Tommy just shook his head in unbelief.

"I just can't believe she would leave like that; in the dead of night and not tell a soul where she was headed!"

Horace Barker voiced everyone's surprise. The stout blacksmith shook his head sadly as he continued. "My girl, Eliza, cried herself to sleep tonight." He sighed, then lifted his foamy mug of beer to his mustache and drank a deep gulp of the amber liquid.

Tim spoke from his seat at the end of the bar. "Yep, she sure took a fancy to the little ones!" He sipped from his glass of whiskey and looked thoughtful. "My guess is she rode out with those miners who were headed off down south last night. They had an extra pack horse along, I recall."

"Do you suppose she was ashamed of those scars?" asked Mrs. Brewer, the gray-haired matron who ran the mercantile with her quiet husband. "She was such a beautiful woman before that. It was such a pity!"

Samuel, who'd arrived after the search, sat next to Kate, with his arm around her. She'd been quiet all evening but now spoke up.

"It was Jack's death that sent her away. Most everyone knew they were in love, I reckon." She lifted her trembling chin. "It is my guess that his death was more than she could bear, even here amongst her friends." Kate couldn't hold back her tears as she said, "Josie Pye was my dearest friend, and I will miss her sorely."

An assenting murmur rose in the room. It seemed everyone felt the same.

"There must be something we can do to honor her for all she's done for us," Chris said. "Several weeks ago, Tim and I started a collection for her at the bakery. With Jack gone, we thought she could use the money, maybe to buy her own place." He held up a leather pouch. "There's two hundred dollars here!"

Samuel rubbed his short, scrubby beard thoughtfully, and then said, "We really can't go after her. If she needed to leave, then we should respect that. I can inquire about her on my routes, and when I find out where she's at, we can see that she gets the money. If we find her, that is."

The assembly thought this was a good idea, and discussed it as they sipped their drinks by the flickering light of the fireplace.

Suddenly, Mr. Jenkins spoke up. "Remember last fall when we were talking of what name to give the mountain peak east of town? How's about we name it Silverheels Mountain, after Josie. Even though she blushed whenever we called her that, I think she was happy with the nickname."

Kate shushed the room and declared, "I think that is a fine and fitting tribute to our Josie!"

So it was decided that night to rename the graceful peak that rose high above the valley between Fairplay and Alma. Anyone who looked at Silverheels Mountain remembered the beautiful young woman who had lost both her true love and her beauty to smallpox. Her acts of kindness were taught to generations of children, and her name was spoken of with respect.

ELEVEN

OVER A YEAR LATER, after Kate and Samuel had been married for several months and were expecting a child, Kate overheard a miner talking to his companion while dining at the hotel. He told of seeing a woman that day, kneeling in the graveyard outside of town.

"It seemed kind of strange, 'cause she was all alone, not even a horse tethered nearby. I was coming down the road from the mine, and I could see her through the trees."

The miner continued eating his dinner, taking large mouthfuls. Kate stepped over and refilled his plate.

"I couldn't help overhearing you," she said, "and I was wondering about the woman you saw in the graveyard. What did she look like?"

The miner stopped chewing, and said, "Ma'am, I can't tell you much about her looks because she was wearin' one of them black veils over her face, the kind that ladies wear in mourning. The wind was blowin' around, and she looked kinda like a ghost. That's what made me notice her in the first place."

That said the stubbly-faced miner turned his attention back to his plate.

Kate thought about the miner's story all evening. Could it have been Josie? Kate stood alone at the sink with her hands in the warm soapy water, absentmindedly wiping the dishes. The clock in the hallway chimed eight times, and Kate came out of her reverie. She wondered when Samuel would be back from the saloon to sit with her.

After their marriage he had given up the stage route and taken over operation of the hotel and saloon. The marriage had been a hasty affair due to the upcoming baby, but both of them were ready for this change in their lives. In spite of her love for Samuel and the excitement of a baby, sadness still clouded her life from the loss of Jack and Josie.

❦

THE NEXT MORNING Kate awoke at sunrise and watched the blue-gray mountains in the east change slowly to a warm pink as the sun touched first the peaks then spread downward like warm molasses. Kate slipped from Samuel's side quietly and dressed. Instead of starting breakfast, she walked toward the graveyard. Soon she entered the cemetery and headed for Jack's grave.

Late February had been warm, and most of the snow had melted from the grassy hummocks that separated the rows of fenced graves. The graveyard was next to a grassy meadow, and the deer and the elk frequented the area. Kate saw fresh hoof prints in the slush.

Kate stepped between the sad rows of small graves with white crosses. All too often babies were stillborn or died a few days after birth. If a baby reached the age of two or three, his chances of survival increased. Kate whispered a fervent prayer for the baby she was carrying.

As she came closer to Jack's grave, she immediately noticed a trail of footprints in the snow. The footprints were small, very likely from a woman's boot, and led to the grave. Nearby, the grass was flattened.

Kate stood in front of the grave and read the carved words.

Jack Herndon
Born 1832 Died 1867

Kate bent down and picked up a small bunch of dried bluebells that lay at the base of the wooden marker. A small string was tied around it.

Josie! Kate looked toward Mosquito Pass. The weather had been mild enough lately for travel. Even for a woman traveling alone.

Kate replaced the flowers with a sigh. Jack would have loved them, she thought. She walked back down the hill through the hummocks and felt Jack and Josie's presence again.

Just as quickly as it came, she felt it slip away on the chill morning breeze that whipped across her face and stung her eyes.

The green pine trees danced against the deep blue Colorado sky. Silverheels Mountain floated above the valley draped in a shining cloak of white. Kate breathed deeply and thought of Samuel. He was surely awake by now and starting the coffee in the kitchen. He would be wondering where she was. Kate felt a flutter and laid her hand on her belly. She smiled in excitement for it was the first time she had felt her baby move.

Kate looked up at the mountain peaks and whispered to the wind, "Life's a river, and we are but leaves upon it." She remembered the words she had spoken almost two years ago. Who knew what life held in store? She smiled and patted her belly. She turned and walked briskly toward Buckskin Joe.

Epilogue

In 1859 the discovery of a rich vein of gold on a branch off the Middle Fork of the South Platte River brought prospectors flooding into the area. The town of Buckskin Joe was located two miles west of Alma, Colorado. The town is said to be named after a Joseph Higgenbottom, a colorful and popular mulatto trapper who wore buckskin clothing. By 1861 the population of Buckskin Joe was estimated to be between five or six hundred, with many more miners working in the outlying areas. Horace Tabor ran a mercantile in Buckskin Joe before moving to Leadville where he struck it rich and became know as the 'Silver King'. In 1862 Buckskin Joe became the County Seat. Before mining declined after 1863, the infamous Phillips Lode was said to have produced over $300,000 worth of gold.

Today no structures stand in Buckskin Joe—all visible traces of the human inhabitants of this once lively mining town are gone except for a gold arrastra and the graveyard. The courthouse building from Buckskin Joe is now located in Fairplay at the South Park City Museum in Park County, Colorado.

Most myths have some kernel of truth behind them, and the story of Silverheels is based on the hamlet of Buckskin Joe, near the town of Alma, Colorado (opposite and on pages 120-121). These photographs are all that remain of the historic underpinnings of the Silverheels legend.

Horace Tabor's General Store at Buckskin Joe, Colorado, above.
The Silverheels Dance Hall in Buckskin Joe taken in 1950, below.

About the Author

Tara Meixsell lives outside of Fairplay, Colorado, with her horses, cats, llamas, and family. She holds a Bachelor of Arts degree in History and Literature from Reed College and an International Montessori Teaching Degree. Tara is a native of Sudbury, Massachusetts, and has been a Montessori teacher in Colorado for ten years. She is currently working on her second book, also a historical novel based in Colorado.